ESCAPE!

IAIN ROB WRIGHT

WANT FREE BOOKS?

Don't miss out on your FREE Iain Rob Wright horror starter pack. Five free bestselling horror novels sent straight to your inbox. No strings attached.

Full Details at the back of book.

Dedicated to all those deeply confused by Brexit.

MIDNIGHT

HELLO! Are you still there? Please come. He left me in the woods. I'm... I'm going to try and find the road. I think I hear a car. Please come.

1

CHAPTER ONE

"HEY CHER, FANCY DOING ME A FAVOUR?"

Cheryl glanced away from her screen and saw Maggie from Accounts standing over her shoulder with her hands on her hips and double D's thrust forward. The woman liked attention. "Oh, um, sure, Mag, what's up?"

"D'you hear about the work thing this weekend? You heard, right, the weekend thing?"

"You mean the company getaway I wasn't invited to? Nope, not sure what you're referring to."

Maggie grimaced, then glanced left and right as if checking the coast was clear. She spoke in a low voice, barely audible over the background din of clacking keyboards and the monotonous chorus of: *Alscon Tiles, how can I help you?* "I agree it was harsh," she said, "but there were only six places to fill. John had to pick names at random."

Bullshit, thought Cheryl. John had picked his best buddies to go, like Monty, the company's top salesman. Funny, how he ended up being one of those 'random' names. Did Mag think she was an idiot?

She thinks everyone's an idiot. That's her problem.

Cheryl's chewed fingernails hovered over the keyboard, eager to get back to work. "So, what's this favour, Mag? I'm kinda busy."

Maggie licked her lips. Her flushed cheeks dimpled. "Would you take my place at the getaway? Pretty please? Say yes!"

Cheryl raised an eyebrow and swivelled in her chair to face Maggie properly. A waft of sickly perfume hit her in the face but she ignored it. "Huh? Why aren't you going?"

"Andrew got us tickets to see *Wicked* for our fifteenth anniversary. Can you believe I've been married that long? Makes me feel totally old. Anyway, he meant it as a surprise but it clashes with this company thing. It's a complete headache, to be honest. I never even wanted to go, but John insisted."

I bet he did! Cheryl didn't voice the thought and feigned irritation instead. "Oh great! You don't want to go on some cheesy work weekend but you expect me to?"

Maggie pouted and placed her manicured fingernails together in mock prayer. "I'm begging you, Cher. If I cancel at the last minute, John'll have a fit, but if I tell him I arranged for you to take my place he won't be able to say anything. Please, please, please! You'll be doing me such a biggie. I'll do whatever you want in return."

"Oo-er!" came a voice from the next cubicle. Leo, the purchasing manager, peered over the partition wall with a smirk on his face. He had a habit of doing that lately, and Cher spent her days never knowing when he would pop up like a meerkat. Today he was wearing a bright green tie decorated with little lions and tigers. It was awful. "Sounds like things are about to get interesting," he said. "Nice!"

"Stay out of it you!" said Maggie, pointing a finger at his crooked nose. Everything about Leo was mildly crooked. He had bony cheeks either side of a ridged nose, and a pair of projecting eyebrows — yet he wasn't bad looking. Somehow his individually harsh features worked in harmony. He was about the same age as Cheryl too.

Just a pity about his slimy personality.

To prove her thought, Leo leered at her, and she didn't know if it was in jest or if he was actually trying to imagine her tits underneath her blouse. "Just say you'll come, Cher. It'll be a laugh."

Maggie bounced excitedly like a grinning moron. She obviously thought two against one was a sure-fire win — and it was true because Cheryl could feel the peer pressure closing in on her and trapping her inside her tiny cubicle. She sighed. "Look, what is this thing? I stopped paying attention when I wasn't invited."

Leo climbed up on his desk so he could hang all the way over the partition wall. He spoke in a hushed, conspiratorial tone. "It's an escape room."

Cheryl frowned. "Like what rich people have in their mansions?"

Leo snorted. "No, Cher, that's a panic room. You're so funny."

"Yeah, okay, whatever. So what is it then? Because it sounds stupid."

Leo suddenly grew serious, which made his thick eyebrows project even further. "It's a game. All of us get locked up in a room, right, and we have to solve a bunch of puzzles, right, and if we escape in less than ninety minutes, we win a grand in cash — each! John is well excited, which makes a change. It was all he could talk about down the Goose last night."

Cheryl groaned. "And that there is the reason I don't want to go. You're all buddies, aren't you? But John and I barely talk. I think he forgot he even hired me. I'm just the mousey girl who sits in the corner of the office all day."

Leo smirked. "What is it you do exactly, Cher? I honestly forgot."

"Yeah, I'm not too sure either," said Maggie with an embarrassed look on her face.

"Are you two serious? I've worked here for three months!" When they continued staring at her blankly, she grunted. "Fine! I run the company's social media and web content, okay? All our advertising too. Does *anybody* appreciate me around here?"

"*I* appreciate you," said Maggie, giving her best attempt at being earnest. Her pink lips and unbuttoned blouse made it somewhat farcical. "And I'll appreciate you even more if you go on this weekend for me. You'll have fun, I promise. Happy's going, so you know everybody will behave themselves."

Cheryl glanced across the room, past the many cubicles arranged in rows. Happy — or Howard Moss, if you used his real name — was the office manager. He was currently standing near the fire exit, tacking another of his 'motivational' posters to the wall. He was the dad of the office, and the thought of him being on the getaway did make her feel better, but it still didn't make spending an entire weekend with her colleagues any more appealing.

But there was that matter of a thousand pounds.

A deposit on a flat. A nice flat.

Or a car. I could actually go places besides work.

She had known nothing about any prize money until Leo had mentioned it, but it was reason enough to endure one awkward weekend. "Fine," she said. "I'll take your place, Mag, but check with John first, okay? Last thing I want is to turn up unexpectedly."

Maggie clapped her hands together and bounced on the spot. Her breasts wobbled beneath her blouse and attracted

Leo's gaze. "Thank you, thank you, thank you! You won't regret this, Cher. I owe you one."

"Yeah, you do!" Cheryl turned back to her screen, hoping it would prompt them to leave her alone. Maggie took the hint and left with a friendly wave, but Leo carried on hanging over the partition wall like a bored child. When she made eye-contact with him, he grinned. "Always knew I'd get you away for a weekend eventually." He winked at her. "If you play your cards right, we might be trapped together all night."

"Trust me," she said, curling her upper lip, "I'll be doing everything I can to escape as quickly as possible. And not just because of the thousand-pound prize."

"Ouch," said Leo. "No need to be like that, Cher-bear. You'll love me once you get to know me, you'll see."

"Or maybe I'll *hate* you worse than I do now. And don't call me Cher-bear, I hate it!" It came out more harshly than she'd intended, and Leo appeared wounded by the jab. He fiddled with his tie and looked away. "Sorry," she added. "I never was any good at the old office banter."

"The problem is," he said, "you're *too* good at it. Excuse me while I remove my battered ego from your presence, princess."

He slid back down into his own cubicle, leaving Cheryl to wonder if she had actually hurt his feelings. The last thing she needed was going into a locked room with someone pissed off with her.

Did I just make an enemy?

She left-clicked the photograph on her monitor and began cropping it ready for the new company catalogue. It was a team shot, featuring the entire staff of Alscon in a group huddle. Cheryl was in the picture, but right at the back, barely visible amongst her smiling, confident co-workers.

Why do I never seem to fit in anywhere? she asked herself. *Why do I feel like a tadpole in a pond full of fish?*

7

She didn't have an answer.

"Do I need to make you sandwiches, sweetheart? I could put some of last night's spaghetti in Tupperware for you."

Cheryl was busy bunching her almond-brown hair into a loose ponytail ready for the weekend. She had also dressed practically in a thick tartan shirt and light-denim jacket. Warm but not sweaty. "No, mum!" she said for the umpteenth time. "I don't need you to make me sandwiches. Jeez, I'm twenty-three. Anyway, this thing is fully catered."

"But you don't want to be eating food you haven't seen prepared. I'll pack you some sarnies just to be safe."

Cheryl stood from the kitchen's small oak table and gave her increasingly frail old ma a hug in front of the Aga. The heat coming off it was comforting, and conjured memories of sitting on the tiles as a child and playing with her dolls. If one thing made her think of home, it was heat from an Aga. "Stop fretting, mum. It's just a weekend — a work thing — I'll be fine."

"What kind of work locks their employees in a room?"

Cheryl chuckled. An escape room must have sounded ludicrous to her sixty-seven-year-old mother — it sounded bizarre enough to herself — but she'd given her word now, and it wasn't worth the hassle of cancelling at the last minute. "It's just a game, mum. Like that show you and dad used to watch on the games channel. The, um, *Crystal Maze*, right? We'll work together to get out of a room by solving puzzles. It's a team building thingy."

Her mother crossed her arms and appeared no less concerned. Since Cheryl's father died two years ago, things had been difficult at home. The sudden loss had all but crippled her mother, and it was heartbreaking to witness, but Cheryl was grieving too. She'd lost her dad before her twenty-second birthday, and her mother's helplessness was becoming a burden. He had always been such an imposing figure, a self-made businessman and a workaholic most of the time, but a loving and warm joker the rest. Without his presence, life had fallen into a depressing stasis, and as much as Cheryl was loath to admit it, the notion of a company outing had grown on her. It was the first weekend she'd had plans in over a month.

I'm supposed to be in my own place by now with a boyfriend and plans for a future. Now it feels like I don't even have a future.

"Have you made a list of everything you need to pack?" Her mother asked, speaking between nibbles at her thumbnail.

"I'm *already* packed, mum. I've got everything I need, I promise. Stop fretting."

"What about Vaseline?"

"What?"

Her mother rooted through one of the kitchen drawers and pulled out a small steel tin, then handed it to Cheryl as if its purpose was obvious. "It's going to be minus-one this afternoon. You know how bad your lips get when it's cold."

Cheryl didn't expect to be spending much time outdoors, but her mother was clearly desperate to be useful. Taking the Vaseline was a tiny gesture, so she reached out and accepted it, sliding the tin into her jean pocket. "Thanks mum. I'll use it if I need it."

Her mother finally relaxed. She leaned back against the Aga's silver handrail. "I don't mean to nag, but you're my baby and I just —"

A honking horn made them both flinch. Cheryl's mother didn't recover from the fright, and her sallow face hung like a Basset Hound. The weight of her worry dragged her pasty grey eyelids downwards. Would she ever stop being such an anxious mess?

I can't live at home forever, mum. I won't.

The car horn honked again.

Cheryl moved towards the door. "That'll be Leo. He's giving me a lift."

Her mother hurried after her like she planned to stop her leaving. "And how long have you known this Leo?"

"Since I started at Alscon."

"Did you leave me the address for the hotel? You said it's more than an hour away."

Cheryl gave her mother another quick hug. "Mum, stop worrying. Leo works in the cubicle next to mine, and he's a nice guy. I've written everything you need to know and put it on the fridge, okay? I have my mobile, and I'll be back tomorrow afternoon. Enjoy some privacy for a couple days. Read a book or something."

"What on earth would I want to read about?"

"I don't know, mum. Maybe try reading something interesting. Who knows, you might actually enjoy yourself."

"Don't be so mean."

Cheryl leaned forward and kissed her mother's forehead. "Sorry, mum."

"Will you just remember to—"

The car horn beeped again, and Cheryl decided not to prolong the moment any further. "I best get going, mum. I'll call you tonight, okay? Love you."

"Love you too, sweetheart. Um, just... keep warm, okay?"

Cheryl hurried out the kitchen's side door and rushed out the front gate. It had been a goodbye far harder than it should've been, which left her frustrated, and yet she was excited too. She was going to have a little fun for one weekend. Was that too much to ask? Besides, it was only a work thing. What was the worst that could happen?

The journey started awkwardly. Leo was chatty, as always, but the general line of conversation oscillated between bad jokes and worse innuendos. Cheryl hadn't known him long, which meant she spent most of the time laughing awkwardly and not knowing how to take things. In the last ten minutes though, Leo had started to settle down, and his words gradually matured to match his age.

"So you still live at home with your mum, huh?" he asked her as they cruised along the dual carriageway at eighty. She wished he'd do seventy.

She had been warming her hands on the dashboard vent, but she sat back now and looked at him. "Yeah, I was planning to move out by now but my, um, dad died of a heart attack a couple years back. It was sudden, you know? He was fit as a fiddle, so it came out of nowhere. Didn't seem right leaving Mum on her own after such a shock."

"I'm sorry, I didn't know."

She shrugged. "Why would you? He died suddenly. Mum still hasn't come to terms with it, really. Not sure she ever will. They were married for over forty years."

Leo glanced away from the road to look at her. His cheeky visage dropped, and she thought she saw genuine sympathy on his face — and why had she not noticed how dark and brown his eyes were before? They were like pools of chocolate. "Both my parents are still around," he said, "but my mum's brother died a few years back from cancer and it really ripped her apart. I thought she was going to get committed at one point, so I get how you needed to look after your mum. It's good of you. Don't know many of our age who would."

"Come on, I'm sure most would. You can't turn your back on your parents, can you?"

Leo raised an eyebrow at that. He refocused on the road

and several minutes passed before he turned back to her again. "So, you been looking forward to this weekend, Cher?"

"No, not at first. I was annoyed at Maggie for landing it on me. I could use a grand though, so I hope we win. You ever done one of these things before, Leo?"

He shook his head. "I watched a few clips on YouTube. They look a good laugh."

"What made John book it? Seems random."

"Don't ask me. He isn't exactly an imaginative guy, so it surprised me too. Maybe an ad popped up while he was watching porn."

Cheryl let out a snort, then covered her nose in embarrassment. "Aren't you and John, like, best mates?"

"No way, *Pedro*! John's twice my age. I think he gets a kick out of hanging out with me down the pub and convincing himself he's still young. Look, I like the guy, don't get me wrong, but we're not as close as people think. Doesn't hurt getting along with the boss though, you know what I mean? When I started at Alscon, I was a warehouse worker. Now I'm head of purchasing. It's not *what* you know, it's *who* you know."

"Tell me about it! It's so cliquey at work. You, Maggie, and all the sales guys speak your own language. I swear I catch you laughing at me sometimes."

"What? You're paranoid, Cher." He gave her a warm smile to back up his claim, drilling into her with those deep brown eyes again. "No one laughs at you."

She frowned, wondering if it was true. Was she paranoid? It had certainly been a while since she'd trusted anyone. Losing her dad so suddenly had made the thought of relying on anyone too much to bear. "Really? It's in my head?"

"Absolutely. You're right though, it *is* cliquey at work. You can thank Maggie for that. I don't think she ever means it, but she can be a real bitch."

Cheryl laughed again, and this time didn't stop herself. "She's like the office mean girl — all smiles to your face and frowns at the back of your head. She kind of intimidates me."

Leo looked away from the road again, and it appeared he was weighing up whether to say something. "You know she and John were a thing for a while, right? He even paid for those *fun bags* of hers. 'Christmas Bonus', he put it down as."

"I've heard rumours they used to be an item, but I try not to involve myself in that type of talk."

At least when it involves my boss.

"Yeah, me too, usually, but when it comes to people getting their rocks off, I like to know all the gory details. With diagrams if possible."

Cheryl grimaced, but ended up chuckling. "You're such a perv."

Leo kept talking. "Apparently, John came on a little strong, so Maggie broke it off. That's what she told me, anyway."

Cheryl folded her hands in her lap and tried to resist getting drawn into gossip, but she feared that if she didn't, the conversation would turn awkward again. "Aren't they both married?"

Leo beeped his horn as somebody, who must have been going a hundred miles an hour, cut in front of them from the right-hand lane. The conversation fizzled as Leo was forced to concentrate on the road so Cheryl listened to the radio for a while. The DJ was running a call-in about football, which instantly made her think about her dad again. They had held twin season tickets each year, and gone to support their team at every home game. Back then, she would've described herself as an avid football fan, but now she realised it had been the time spent with him that she had loved. Her interest in football had died with him.

Another twenty minutes passed, and then Leo turned off

the main highway and entered a narrow access road that rapidly turned from tarmac to gravel. They followed that for ten minutes until they spotted a group of ramshackle farm buildings.

Cheryl leaned forward in her seat, trying to get a better view through the windshield. "D'you think this is the place?"

Leo tapped his slender fingers on top of the steering wheel and peered out of his side window as they trundled along the gravel road. "According to the Sat Nav, it is. I was expecting something a little more... less of a farm."

"Yeah, me too. Then again, lots of farms have petting zoos and stuff attached nowadays, don't they?Maybe there's not enough money in just being a farm anymore. It's sad."

"Blame the supermarkets for putting the squeeze on agricultural profits."

"Seriously, is that the reason?"

He shrugged. "I dunno. Did it make me sound smart?"

"Um, not anymore..."

Leo pulled the car into a muddy patch outside a steel shack full of hay, and they both spotted the bonnet of John Alscon's silver Bentley peeking out from the other side of the bales. Each morning, when Cheryl passed the luxury motor parked outside the office, she thought it was boxy and ugly — not something she would spend money on even if she had it — but she supposed the main thing was the badge on the bonnet.

Leo brought his car to a stop and yanked the handbrake which made a loud *kwunk*! Then he switched off the engine and gurned at Cheryl. "Time to get this party started, Cher-bear!"

She couldn't help but loose a smile. He was taking this so seriously, like he planned on making it the best weekend ever. "Just behave yourself," she told him. "Or we'll leave you behind in the escape room."

"You'll be begging to stay with me by tonight, I promise."

"Keep dreaming."

Both chuckling, they exited the car and stepped into the mud. Cheryl wished she'd worn boots instead of the gleaming white trainers she'd chosen in anticipation of being indoors. The last thing she needed was an embarrassing slip in front of her colleagues. As her mother had warned, it was chilly, and she had to pull her denim jacket tightly around herself to keep warm. She let out an obligatory, *Brrr!*

John emerged from behind his Bentley, dressed in a Burberry jacket and matching flat cap. He waved to greet them, but then stopped and frowned. "Cheryl? What are *you* doing here?"

She cleared her throat and fidgeted with the buttons on her denim cuff. "Um, didn't Maggie tell you? She couldn't make it."

John's frown lingered a moment more before he glanced to the side. "But Maggie's right *here*."

Maggie stepped out from behind the Bentley, dressed in purple furry boots, purple furry coat, and purple furry hat. She appeared embarrassed, chuckling like an idiot. "OMG," she said, putting her mittened hands against her cheeks. "I totally forgot, Cher! I'm such an idiot. Wow, I can't even..."

Leo moved away from Cheryl as if a rotten smell had suddenly emanated from her. She had a feeling she was about to hear something she wouldn't much appreciate. "What the hell, Maggie? You said you couldn't make it. Theatre tickets?"

Maggie shook her head, making the tassels on her woollen hat swing back and forth like pendulums. "The tickets Steve bought are for *next* weekend, can you believe it? I'm such a scatterbrain. I can't believe I forgot to tell you, Cher."

Cheryl took two steps forwards, then realised she was clenching her fists. It took an effort to open them again. "I've just driven an hour with Leo to get here, Maggie. I've packed a bag and cancelled my other plans."

Nobody needed to know she'd had no other plans.

Maggie's sheepish grin finally fell, but she only gave a shrug. "Sorry, Cher. Really, I am."

Cheryl took another step forward, fists re-clenching. Was Maggie even hearing her? "Seriously? That's all you've got to say? Jesus!"

John stepped in front of Maggie protectively and held a leather-gloved hand up to Cheryl in a way she didn't much like, but as dismissive as the gesture was, he didn't seem upset. In fact, he looked disappointed by the mix-up. "Look," he said, walking over and putting a leather-gloved hand on her lower back. "I'm sure we can squeeze an extra person in, Cheryl. They specifically stated six, but you're here now, aren't you? Even if you can't take part in the escape room, you can at least stay at the hotel and have fun with the rest of us. We're not going to send you back home by yourself. That would be wretched of us."

Maggie smiled and clapped her hands together. "See! It's all worked out for the best."

Cheryl sighed. She was still angry but couldn't see the virtue in remaining that way. She was there to have fun. "Thanks John. This is really embarrassing."

He removed his hand from her back and gave her a smile. "Don't be silly, Cher. I'm glad you're here. More the merrier."

"I'm glad you're here too," said Leo, and he glared at Maggie to show whose side he was on. He even muttered the word *idiot*, which caused Maggie's eyes to widen as if he'd just called her something unforgivable.

Cheryl rolled her eyes. *Drama queen.*

John broke the tension by changing the subject. He had lost much of the formal tone he used at work, and Cheryl was amused to find that he had a mild Bristolian accent. "So, Leo? You find this place all right?"

"Yeah, boss, no probs whatsoever." He trudged over to John and gave him a 'man hug' complete with pats on the back and ample groin distance between them. "Where are the others?"

John nodded over Leo's shoulder toward the gravel road. "Looks like them now."

Cheryl turned to see a tall black Range Rover bouncing down the gravel road. Behind the wheel was Monty, the company's top salesman. In the back, sitting alone, was Happy, while Alfie, another lad from sales, sat in the front passenger seat. This was Alscon's inner circle and, somehow, she had found herself right in the middle. The weekend might really help her job prospects.

Or it could be the weekend from hell.

CHAPTER TWO

MONTY — real name Mohammed Rizwan according to the numerous sales awards adorning his desk back at the office — parked his Range Rover and hopped down into the mud. Fully togged in a three-piece suit, Cheryl took pleasure seeing his shiny black loafers get spattered, but she then chided herself for being so mean.

Happy disembarked after Monty, then Alfie clambered out the front passenger side and lit a fag. The three of them marched towards the hay barns like something out of *Reservoir Dogs*.

Bum-bumbum-bumbum-bumbum-bumbum-babum.

Cheryl chuckled to herself, then stood aside as everyone greeted one another. She grew more and more awkward until, eventually, Monty noticed her presence and looked her up and down as if he were judging a poodle at a dog show. He offered his hand and it was ice-cold as she shook it. "You're the new bird doing the computers and stuff, yeah?"

She forced a smile to her face. "John hired me as an online marketer a few months back. I work in the cubicle next to Leo's." She wanted to add that her cubicle was also only ten feet from his, and that there had been ample opportunities for him to welcome her to the team.

"I've seen you plenty, luv. Sorry, we ain't got to know each other yet, but you know how it is with sales, yeah? Gotta stay on the ball or the rabbit gets away."

"Um, yeah, good metaphor. So everyone tells me you're the company's top dog. Is that true?"

Monty did a little head jig and thumbed his cropped beard. She wasn't sure what the gesture represented, but it reeked of arrogance. "I can't comment on what others say about me, luv. I'm just trying to do a job, innit?"

She raised an eyebrow, pretending to be interested in his patter. "So how do you convince people our tiles are the best? What's your secret, Monty?"

He put his hand on her shoulder and looked her right in the eye. His musky cologne irritated her nostrils and made her want to sneeze. "I don't sell tiles, luv. I sell a service, yeah? You buy tiles from Monty Rizwan and you know you're gunna get looked after proper."

Cheryl strained to maintain her polite smile, and it became progressively harder when Monty declined to release her shoulder and kept staring at her intensely. It was like he was trying to hypnotise her, or perhaps he thought he was seducing her. *Gross*!

Eventually John saved her from the awkwardness by clapping his gloved hands together and getting everyone's attention. "Okay," he said. "Monty will give a brief talk at the hotel tonight about how he sells twice as many tiles as everyone else combined, but today we're here to have fun. No work talk, okay? That's an order."

Leo gave a cheer. "Nice!"

"Sounds like a plan," said Happy, although Cheryl imagined his idea of *play* greatly differed to Leo's. Maggie gave a double thumbs-up like a hyperactive school kid and then shoved her hands in her pockets as if she couldn't control them. What was wrong with her today? She'd claimed not to want to even come this weekend, but she was more excited than any of them. Cheryl couldn't help but glare at her.

Is she playing some kind of game? Or has she lost the plot?

"So where is this thing?" asked Alfie between drags on his cigarette. He was the company's junior salesman and John's nephew, and while Cheryl didn't know his exact age, it was possible he was still holding onto teenhood by a month or two. He still sported the odd zit but was hot as hell otherwise. The problem was Alfie knew it and carried himself as if he were putting on a show for the world. His inky-black hair was slick with gel, and only a surgeon's scalpel could have shaped his beard. She considered that his over-confidence might be a defence-mechanism stemming from him having a stunted left hand, which she always found difficult not to stare at. Before Alfie received an answer to his question, he looked at Cheryl and asked another. "How come *you're* here? I thought it was just us six."

Cheryl gave Maggie a sidewards glance. "I think the plan is to smuggle me in."

"That's cool. More pretty ladies the better, innit? And Maggie's already spoken for."

Cheryl noticed the comment caused John and Maggie to glance sheepishly at one another. She assumed Alfie was referring to the fact Maggie was married, but it seemed to imply something else. It might also count as flirting, so she tried her hardest not to blush.

"Isn't somebody supposed to meet us here?" asked Leo. He turned a circle and scanned the farmyard, but all that existed was an old tractor with a slashed tyre and two steel sheds. Beyond that lay only frost-tipped fields and the gravel road. "What's the deal with this place? What are we supposed to do?"

"Oh, forgetful me!" John patted himself down. "I received an envelope of instructions to be opened when we arrived. I suppose now would be a good time."

Leo scoffed. "Um, yeah, boss. Now would be a good time unless you like standing around in the cold waiting for some bumpkin to come murder us."

Alfie frowned. "What the hell's a bumpkin?"

"A yokel," said Happy.

"Oh, okay. What's a yokel?"

Cheryl tittered. "It's someone who lives in the country. Like *really* in the country."

"Oh."

Maggie let out a cackle. "You lot crack me up."

Leo frowned at her, making it obvious that he too thought she was acting weird.

John pulled the envelope from the inside pocket of his Burberry jacket and fingered open the seal. While he was busy, Happy came over to greet Cheryl. The ageing office manager was wrapped in an unfashionable sheepskin coat worn over light-blue jeans. It belied both his advancing age and lack of fashion sense. To top it all off, he wore an over-sized badge on his lapel that read: *NEVER GIVE UP.* "It's a nice surprise to see you here, Cheryl," he said in a thicker version of the Bristolian accent John used. "Unexpected though."

"Unexpected is right," she said. "Maggie said she needed me to take her place then bloody well turns up. Can you believe it?"

Happy sighed. "Unfortunately, yes, that's rather a Maggie thing to do. It wouldn't have been personal, I assure you. She's forgetful at the best of times, especially of late."

"The whole thing is embarrassing."

"I'll bet, but you're here now so there's no escaping it." He chuckled, but then grew serious. "I've been meaning to ask how you're settling in at Alscon. Everything going okay?"

"Yeah, great, thanks. I'm hoping this weekend might help me get to know everyone a little better. It's nice to be a part of things."

He nodded sagely. "Inclusion is key to morale."

"Um, yep." She offered a smile. Motivational epithets were part of Happy's job, but he spouted them so often that they lost meaning. Last week, he'd told her that the key to a successful future was correcting past failures. It was perfectly sound advice, but she'd only been making a cup of coffee at the time.

John unfolded the letter and flapped it out in front of him. "Okay," he said, clearing his throat. "It says, and I quote: *Unburden yourself to reveal your destiny.*" He looked up from the piece of paper. "That's all it says."

"Seriously?" Monty shuffled to keep his loafers out of the mud. "There's gotta be more than that."

John studied the paper again, front and back. "Nope. Nothing. Just that one sentence."

"What if it's, like, invisible ink or something," said Maggie, "like in those old spy films."

Leo smirked. "What spy films have you seen, Mag?"

She shrugged. "Austin Powers."

"Ha! Austin Powers?"

"Never heard of it," said Alfie.

They all chuckled, which led to Maggie blushing. "What? That's a spy film, isn't it?"

Leo shook his head, bemused. "Come on, guys, we need to think about this."

"It's one of those riddle thingys, I reckon," said Alfie. He untied the thick scarf around his neck and redid it tighter. Despite having only one finger and a thumb on his left hand he used it deftly. Once again, Cheryl forced herself not to stare at the unusual appendage.

Ignore the hand. He's a hottie. Just ignore the hand.

I'm going to Hell.

Monty scoffed at Alfie. "State the obvious why don't you, bruh."

Alfie sucked his teeth. "You mugging me off, bruh?"

"Yeah, bruh. What you gunna do about it?"

"I'll knock your block off, bruh, innit?"

John clapped his hands as if trying to break up a dog fight. "Guys!"

"We need to leave our belongings," said Cheryl, ignoring the banter war between the two salesmen and thinking out loud. It gained everyone's attention.

Monty turned to her and somehow managed to belittle her with only a look. "What's that, luv?"

"I was offering an answer to the riddle."

Monty winked at her. "That's the spirit. Now, let Monty have a stab at—"

Leo cut him off. "Cher's right! We're supposed to, I dunno, empty our pockets or whatever."

John studied the paper in his hands and repeated the clue to see if it fit. "*Unburden yourself to reveal your destiny*. It makes sense! I think you're onto something, Cheryl. Good work!"

Cheryl couldn't help but smile. John was twice her age, and a bit of a dick from the little she knew of him, but he was a confident, successful businessman. To have him pleased with her was a nice feeling that she couldn't deny. Even now, John was still smiling at her encouragingly.

The weekend had started well.

Cheryl's nerves began to fade. She was having fun.

After several minutes' searching, Alfie discovered a wicker basket perched atop the hay bales. Inside was a label reading: BELONGINGS (ALL).

Leo nudged Cheryl on the arm. "Looks like you were right. Nice going, Cher-bear."

She grinned. "Yeah, it was *nice*!"

"Okay, everyone," said John, taking on the role of leader. "Pop your stuff in the basket. I'm sure it'll remain safe and sound while we get on with the game."

Alfie looked uneasy. "Even our mobiles, boss?"

"Yes. We have to leave everything."

"It's probably to stop us cheating at the games," said Happy. "Won't be much fun if we can get all the answers from searching on Yahoo."

Leo stifled a laugh and had to look away. It caused Cheryl to do the same.

"What about my fags?" Alfie asked. "I don't want to be trapped in a room gasping for a cigarette."

John grunted. "Then you best help us escape quickly. Fags, phones, and wallets all in the basket, please, everyone."

Alfie did as he was told but made sure to sulk.

Monty produced an obscenely large mobile phone and plonked it in the basket. "I ain't got no signal anyway. They better not scratch it though, I swear down. Seventy-quid a month that costs me, innit?"

"I've left my handbag in the car," said Maggie, glancing at John anxiously. She suddenly seemed less excited. "Maybe I should go get it."

John dangled his car keys and dropped them in the basket. "The key only works with my thumbprint. Your bag will be perfectly secure, don't worry."

"I got to get me one of those," said Monty. "Maybe it's time to upgrade the Range."

Cheryl couldn't tell if he was joking. "Change your car just to get an upgraded key fob?"

Monty frowned at her as though he didn't understand. "The company's top salesman needs the best, innit? People see the bling and want a piece of the action."

"So having a brand new car helps you sell more tiles?"

"Exactly, luv."

Alfie tittered. "Should've seen the penis extension he was driving before he got the Range!"

"Shut your mouth, blud!"

"I didn't bring a phone," said Happy, tossing in only a wallet and a set of keys. "It broke down months ago, and I didn't bother replacing it. I still prefer to view the world with my own eyes instead of through a screen."

Cheryl smiled. It was a nice philosophy, but she wasn't sure she could cope without her phone. Even with few friends, she had it on her constantly — if only to keep pictures of her father close by. She pulled it out of her coat pocket now, along with the small purse she kept her cards in, and prepared to discard it. She expected it to be a freeing act but anxiety took over, and she worried if she should call her mother and let her know she'd arrived safely.

No! She can cope without me for an afternoon. It won't kill her. I'm here to have fun.

Cheryl tossed her belongings into the basket and stepped back. Everyone eventually gathered at the muddy patch of ground where Leo had parked his car. She wasn't great with car badges, but she thought it was a Mazda or a Hyundai. Sitting between the Bentley and Range Rover, it looked rather common.

Alfie threw his dogend on the ground and stamped on it, then flicked a few loose strands of slick black hair behind his ear. "So what now?"

John turned on the spot. Once he'd completed a full circle, he grunted. "I'm not entirely sure."

Maggie was rubbing at her shoulders and shivering, even though she was more warmly dressed than the rest of them. "Are they watching us, d'you think?"

Leo frowned. "What, like, hidden cameras?"

She nodded. "Yeah."

"I don't see any."

"I was told not to expect help," said John. "but I thought they would at least meet us here, or keep an eye on things. What if something goes wrong? They *must* be watching."

Cheryl kept hearing a word, and she asked about it now. "Can I just ask who *they* are exactly?"

John cleared his throat and looked at his gleaming gold watch impatiently. "*They* are an events company, and *they* already explained that the game would be very hands-off as far as supervision went. We're supposed to come together as a team and work this all out. That's the whole point, isn't it?"

Cheryl nodded. It made sense. "Okay, so how did you find this company in the first place?"

"Actually, *they* contacted me. They do corporate functions and want Alscon to sign up for an account. One of their reps came by the office and offered us a weekend free of charge as a way of showing what they can offer."

"So, this isn't costing the company anything?" said Maggie. "What about the hotel?"

"All part of the deal."

"Oh." Maggie seemed dejected. "I don't feel treated anymore."

"Just because it's free doesn't mean it has no value," said Happy. "The fun we'll have shall be no less."

"What fun?" Alfie huffed. "We're standing in the mud like spare pricks at attention. It's cold, man. Is this company even legit? I'm getting a bad vibe about this."

"Yes, they're legit," snapped John. "I had Happy check everything out. It's all above board."

Everyone looked at Happy who shrugged his shoulders innocently. "They had a website and an address. The business checked out with Company's House, too, when I checked. I even called their head office and made some enquiries. This is all just part of the game. I know it feels odd but leaving our comfort zone is exactly what this weekend is about. We should embrace it."

"Whatever, man." Alfie rolled his eyes. "Let's just get on with it because my nuts are freezing."

Cheryl nodded in agreement. She'd already taken to cuddling herself to stay warm, but it wasn't enough to keep out the morning chill. An icy sheen coated the steel frameworks of the farm buildings. This was supposed to be about escaping a room, so why were they standing out in the wilderness?

"Hey, bruh!" Monty shouted up at the tin roof of the hay store. "Whoever's in charge of this thing, help us out, yeah? We've placed all our stuff in the basket. Now what?"

Nobody replied. Cheryl saw no cameras. It didn't feel like anyone was watching.

A car alarm went off. Distant.

Leo frowned. "That isn't coming from our cars."

"It's coming from the fields," said Happy, pointing yonder with a great big grin on his face.

"It's the next step," said John. "We follow that sound and see what we find."

Leo took off into the field, leaving the others with no choice but to follow. "Last one there has an STD!"

Once again, Cheryl wished she'd worn a pair of boots, but there was nothing she could do about it now.

Monty yelled. "Hold up! Shit, man, I'm wearing Gucci loafers."

Cheryl had to cover her mouth to keep from sniggering. Fortunately for Monty, the mud fell away to thick grass and their footing grew surer. The deeper they headed into the field, the louder the car alarm became. After a minute, it caused them to cover their ears.

"We must be close," said Maggie, pressing her mittens against her ears. "I'm getting a headache."

John rolled his eyes. "Try to enjoy yourself, Maggie. You told me you were up for this."

Cheryl followed right behind but couldn't make out what Maggie muttered to John in reply. Were the two of them still carrying on in secret? Or was there a grudge developing? They seemed intolerant of one another.

Proof you shouldn't shit where you eat.

"The alarm is coming from here," said Leo, wheeling around and looking in every direction. "We're right on top of it, I swear."

The grass was particularly long where they now stood, and it left Cheryl with wet jeans around her ankles. She kicked at great clumps of greenery to get at the dirt beneath for, like Leo, she also was certain they were right on top of the noise. A few seconds later, she found something hidden beneath the grass. Or, more to the point, she *tripped* on something hidden in the grass. Her ankle struck an obstacle and she stumbled. Happy had to reach out and steady her. She thanked him.

"A rope," said Leo, pointing at what had tripped her. "There's a rope on the ground."

Monty shuffled over and inspected the ground, then reached down and pulled up the rope with both hands. A great length of it erupted from the earth, tossing up clumps of mud and grass. Inch by inch, Monty slid his hands along the rope, shuffling along and trying to find its origin. All the while, the car alarm continued blaring.

Maggie moaned. "Please shut that wretched thing off."

Alfie pushed his scarf up over his nose and mouth to stay warm. "I don't see a car anywhere."

"It has to be here," said Leo.

Monty reached the end of the rope and alerted the others so that they gathered around. The rope was attached by a hook to something buried in the grass. Monty tugged it twice tentatively, then followed it up with a good hard yank. The ground erupted, and mud and grass spilled over his loafers, making him dance. "Sod it!"

Leo pointed. "It's a trapdoor!"

Monty gave the rope one more yank and a large wooden hatch flipped over to reveal a hole in the earth. The car alarm blared louder.

"This is so cool," said Leo. "I feel like Indiana Jones."

Happy beamed. "Good work, team!"

Cheryl stepped up to the hole and stared down into the darkness. The thought of climbing down into the earth filled her with dread. She'd watched a film once about a child trapped down a well and it had always stayed with her.

"Look," said Alfie, pointing at the hatch lid and alerting them to a message painted on the underside in black tar. It read: ENTER & BEGIN.

"This must be the escape room," said John. "Good work."

"Did you know it was underground?" Cheryl asked uneasily. Her stomach was in knots, and she had to breathe deeply to stay calm. She could not — could not — freak out in front of these people. *It's just a game*, she told herself. *Be a grown up.*

John shook his head at her. "All I knew to expect was a room, and that if we fail to escape it in ninety minutes, a member of staff will release us and take us to the hotel."

Cheryl swallowed a lump in her throat. *An hour-and-a-half trapped underground? Okay, don't freak. Don't freak.*

Everyone glanced around, but there were no members of

IAIN ROB WRIGHT

staff anywhere in view. If they didn't have to be there for over an hour though, they could easily be close enough to get there on time.

Leo placed his hands in his coat pockets and flapped like a bird. "The ninety minutes has probably already started. We should get moving."

Cheryl shivered as a gust of wind buffeted the inside of her denim jacket. "I'm not sure about this."

"Me either," said Alfie, clutching himself in the same way that she was, "and I'm freezing."

"Can we just shut off that bloody alarm?" said Maggie, still covering her ears. "I'm going to have a goddamn epileptic fit."

Leo rolled his eyes. "Not how that works, Maggie."

"I really don't wanna go down there, man," said Alfie, restating his fears.

"Pussy," said Monty. "What you scared of?"

"Your mum's tits. They look like two bags of rice."

"I'm willing to go first," said Happy. "If it will make everyone else less nervous."

Monty kicked dirt off his loafers and stepped up to the hole. "I don't get nervous, bruh. You lot just try to keep up." He took a moment to examine the entrance, then carefully got down on his hands and knees before crawling backwards onto a ladder he found inside. He descended the first couple of rungs, then paused before going any deeper.

"You okay?" Cheryl asked. She had to shout over the car alarm.

Monty smirked at her, but it was an unconvincing display. "Yeah, luv, I'm just enjoying the anticipation, innit? Monty's gunna win this thing, you get me?"

Cheryl wondered if he was panicking. He had stopped abruptly, as if the fear had suddenly seized him. She didn't blame him in the least. "It's not a contest, Monty," she said. "We win or lose this together."

"Keep telling yourself that, luv."

Leo tapped his wrist despite not wearing a watch. "Come on, dude. The clock's a-ticking. Get in the hole."

Monty hesitated one more moment, then got moving again. Soon he disappeared out of sight, hidden beneath the ground. Covered by darkness.

Like a grave.

Happy shouted into the hole after a minute. "Are you okay down there, Monty?"

No reply. Perhaps the car alarm was too loud for him to hear. Likewise, would they be able to hear him if he shouted up to them?

John paced back and forth beside the hole. "Monty? What's down there?" He raised his voice louder over the alarm. "MONTY?"

No answer.

Cheryl's stomach churned. She was both excited and anxious at once. Was it fun she was having? It had been too long to recognise the feeling.

Leo spied the hole suspiciously. "Why isn't he responding?"

"I don't know," said John, hands on his hips. "He best not be pissing around."

Cheryl moved towards the hole. Whatever was down there, she'd rather find out and get it over with. Any more anticipation and she would puke. She peered into the hole but could make out no details besides the dull glint of the ladder's first rungs. "I'll go down."

John looked at her. "You sure?"

She took a deep breath, preparing to descend into the earth. *Here's me having* fun. *See, mum, nothing to worry about.*

Absolutely nothing at all.

A bright light blinded her and she almost stumbled right

into the hole. Leo grabbed her arm and pulled her back just in time. "Whoa! You okay?"

"Yeah! What is that?"

John yelled into the suddenly lit shaft. "Monty, is that you? Did you switch a light on?"

Over the din of the car alarm, Monty finally gave a reply. "Yeah boss, it was me. You need to get down here and see this — and quickly. The clock's ticking, bruh."

<hr />

After almost falling into a hole in the earth, Cheryl's enthusiasm waned. As it was, both Leo and Alfie went down before she did. Happy placed a hand on her back. "You want to go next?"

"Yeah, um, sure." Her nerves had recovered slightly, and she still wanted to get it over with, so she tightened her ponytail, pulled her jacket around herself, and stepped up to the edge of the hole. "Will you help me, Happy?"

"Of course." He offered his arm, and she used it to keep herself steady as she descended onto the first rung of the ladder. It felt hollow and sent vibrations through her foot. As she started down, the car alarm really got inside her skull. Why was it still blaring? Had Monty not discovered the source? If not, then what had got him so excited?

My head is about to explode.

After descending several more rungs, a hand landed on her back and caused her to yelp. "It's okay," Leo assured her over the blaring car alarm. "You're at the bottom."

She looked down and saw the ground two-feet below her. Descending one more rung, she hopped onto a metal floor. The echoless thud of her landing was ominous, and when she peered back up the ladder, she estimated she was fifteen feet underground.

"Look at this place!" Alfie shouted. "Look at it!"

She turned away from the ladder to see what all the fuss was about and found herself inside a tunnel constructed from half-a-dozen shipping containers placed end-to-end. Separate rooms lay off to each side, their entrances sliced into the steel walls of the containers and barred with gates. A line of bulbs swung overhead and gave light while hot air pumped in from somewhere near their feet. In several places between the lights, fan blades rotated sluggishly, letting in clean air. Remarkable. "How on earth did they get all this underground?"

Leo shrugged. "It's only a few buried shipping containers welded together."

"Oh, come on. This place is impressive, admit it!"

"Yeah, okay, I suppose it is pretty cool. They must have built it first and then put soil over the top."

"It's well sweet," said Alfie. "I didn't expect anything like this."

Maggie stepped off the ladder to join them and then immediately covered her ears. John and Happy arrived moments later. They were all inside now.

Fifteen feet underground in the middle of nowhere.

"We have to shut off that noise," moaned Maggie. The lids beneath her eyes had gone an unhealthy charcoal, and her luscious lips appeared dry. Perhaps she really did have a headache. She certainly looked ill all of a sudden.

The ladder down which they had climbed was not against the rear wall of the container, and there was, in fact, space behind it. Cheryl's ears told her the alarm was coming from that alcove.

"So what have you found?" John asked as he slipped his flatcap off his head and stuffed it into one of his jacket's over-sized pockets. His brown hair was unkempt and slightly sweaty as he patted it down.

"I switched the lights on here." Monty tapped a lever on the wall and shoved it upwards. The lights went out. Darkness smothered them. Cheryl swallowed a lump in her throat and wished she'd eaten more for breakfast. Yet, despite the darkness, she wasn't completely blind. A single, luminous word floated in the shadows. It read: PULL.

The lights flicked back on. Monty still had his hand on the lever, but now it was in the down position. "That word was the only thing I could see when I got down here," he explained, "so I felt around until I found this lever. Soon as the lights came on that clock started ticking down."

They all looked at where Monty was pointing. On the opposite wall was a large digital clock with bright red numbers.

86:45

86:44

86:43

Cheryl groaned, feeling a thousand pounds slipping away from her second by second. "We have less than an hour-and-a-half to escape."

Tick. Tick. Tick.

"But we could escape right now," said Leo, pointing up at the square opening fifteen feet above their heads. He moved in front of the ladder and placed his hands on either side. "Aren't we supposed to be locked-in? I mean, we could just climb right back—" He stepped onto the first rung and a whole section of the ladder came away from its moorings. He let out a cry and staggered backwards as the entire lower length fell apart. The pieces clattered against the steel floor and everyone had to back up against the wall to keep from being struck. Alfie got hit on the shin and hissed. "What the effin hell!"

Maggie growled and pressed her fingers against her temples over her wooly hat. "This is ridiculous."

Everyone stared at the broken ladder, then at each other. What had just happened? Did something go wrong? Had it been an accident?

Leo gawked at the disembodied section of ladder still in his hands. "I could've cracked my bloody head open."

Cheryl stared up at the hatch. It was suddenly much further away than fifteen feet. Only the top few rungs of the ladder remained in place, the other pieces all scattered across the floor. A thick steel cable swung in the air just out of reach. Had it been holding the ladder together? She looked back at the clock and wondered if it had been rigged to a timer or set to self-destruct as soon as someone tried to climb back up it. Maybe it was just shoddy maintenance.

"Well, it looks like we're good and trapped now," said John, glaring at Leo. "Nice going."

"You're going to blame *me* for that?"

"It was clumsy."

"Yeah, excuse me for being a clumsy ladder climber."

"It's part of the game," said Happy, trying to keep the peace like he always did. "The ladder was obviously designed to collapse, but what you said is right, John. We're trapped. The game has begun."

"Can we please shut off that car alarm?" Maggie begged, still clutching her head. "I can't take it anymore. I can't take another second."

"Don't get hysterical," John chided.

"Screw you, John!"

He whirled on her, a flash of anger on his face. Happy put a hand up before any more words were spoken. "Come on, you two. We're here to have fun."

Cheryl avoided the tension by moving to the space where the ladder had been. "I think the alarm is coming from back here," she said. "I'll take a look."

Everyone stood by while she investigated the alcove. A

35

curtain hung from a rail, and she slid it aside to discover the front half of a bright red sports car. The headlights flashed to life and made the paintwork appear even brighter. The alarm was definitely coming from somewhere beneath the car's sleek metal bonnet. "Wow!" she said. "That's an expensive prop. Is it a Ferrari?"

"A TVR," said Alfie, then glanced at Monty.

"Oh, well, it's beautiful. Don't think I'll ever get to drive one. I'm still saving up for a Mini."

"Honesty is the key to peace," said Leo, and when everyone looked at him quizzically, he pointed to a sign on the wall above the driver's side. The sign read, in bold typeface: HONESTY IS THE KEY TO PEACE.

"What d'you think it means?" Leo asked.

"It's another riddle," said Happy. "Any ideas?"

Cheryl wracked her brain but nothing came immediately to mind, so she searched for further clues. After a moment, she was forced to shout at the others over the din of the alarm. "Come on, you lot. Get looking. Time is money."

Everyone snapped to attention and joined the search. Cheryl peered beneath the car but saw only smooth cement. The two front tyres were flat, but she could find nothing strange about them. She had no clue what she was looking for, and the noise of the alarm was making it difficult to think.

"Open the bonnet," said Maggie. "Disconnect that alarm, for the love of God!"

Leo nodded. "Maybe that's what we're supposed to do."

"I don't care what we're supposed to do, just do it!"

"Okay, Mag, jeez! What's wrong with you today?"

"Nothing! I'm just getting a migraine."

John frowned. "You don't get migraines."

"I do today."

"The horn is usually a wire attached to the battery," said

Happy. He stepped forward and tugged at the lip of the bonnet. It popped up easily on an automatic hinge and an impressive-looking engine glared back at them. Blue pipework and thick wires streaked back and forth above a thick slab of metal. Cheryl knew nothing of engines, but she could tell this one was a beast. The odd thing about it was the tablet device affixed to the top.

The rectangular screen flashed to life and displayed a message. Cheryl read it aloud with a chuckle, for it was a mildly cheeky question. "*What is the combined age of your group?*"

"Ooh," said Alfie. "No blagging, you lot."

"I'm twenty-five," said Monty with a shrug.

"Fifty-three," said Happy.

Alfie grinned. "Young, free, and nineteen, innit?"

"Twenty-four," said Leo before adding, "and a half."

Cheryl gave her answer without embarrassment. She was at a convenient age where she felt neither too young nor too old. "Twenty-three."

That left John and Maggie, both of which looked at one another awkwardly. "Well, um," John began, peeling off his leather driving gloves and placing them in his pocket as he spoke. "I hope I don't look it, but I'm forty-four."

"I'm thirty-seven," said Maggie, looking pissed off at having to answer. "My birthday was last June."

"Okay," said Leo, "so altogether that's—" His eyes rolled upward as he did the math in his head. "—two-hundred-and-twenty-five, right?"

Cheryl shrugged. "Don't ask me. You want me to type it in?"

John nodded. "Yes, type it in Cheryl. There's a good girl."

Cheryl moved a finger towards the tablet's touchscreen. Below the question was a little box, and when she tapped it a number pad popped up. She entered their answer: **2-2-5**.

The car alarm stopped.

Maggie sighed. "Oh, thank you, thank you!"

The car alarm restarted.

A red X flashed on the tablet before the screen reset and presented the same question about age. Everyone groaned — Maggie loudest of all. Alfie looked at Leo accusingly. "Did we do the math right?"

Leo didn't take offence, and quickly took everyone's ages again. He arrived at the same answer. "I'm sure it's two-hundred-and-twenty-five," he said. "Maybe Cher put the wrong number in."

"I didn't!" She had snapped at him a little for she was already annoyed at having been called a 'good girl' by John.

"Just try it again, please," asked John, but it sounded like an order. Perhaps they hadn't truly left work behind.

She tapped in the code a second time.

The alarm stopped.

The screen flashed a red X and the alarm resumed.

Everyone gave a second groan.

"This is rigged," said Alfie, shaking his head in disgust.

"No, wait!" said Happy. "It's because of Cheryl."

"Hey! I'm just putting in the number you guys are telling me to."

Happy shook his head. "No, no, I mean you're not supposed to be here. The answer would have been pre-programmed, probably before we arrived. There's only meant to be six of us. We smuggled you in."

John clicked his fingers at Happy. "You're right! I had to give everybody's details when I first booked this thing. It didn't include Cheryl."

"Thanks for reminding me."

"Okay," said Leo, "so Two-hundred-and-twenty-five minus twenty-three is... two-hundred-and-two, right?"

Cheryl wasted no time. She tapped in the new answer.

2-0-2

A red X flashed up on screen. The alarm continued.

"Okay, I'm done," said Maggie. "I quit. Get me out of here. This is horrible."

"Someone's lying," said Leo. "That's the only thing it can be. Someone isn't telling the truth."

They all looked at Maggie.

"Hey," she said with a growl. "I told the truth. I'm thirty-seven."

Alfie smirked. "Come on, Mag. We're all friends here. I think you left thirty-seven in the rearview a while back. Just admit it, you've had work done, right?"

"How dare you!"

"It's me," said John, staring at the ground. "I lied. I'm forty-nine."

Maggie gawped at him. "You're kidding me? You're almost fifty?"

"You look good for your age," said Cheryl, and it was true. John still had thick brown hair with only a hint of grey at the temples. He was also slim with a thick set of shoulders. He could probably pass for forty on a good day.

Maggie glared at Cheryl, then turned to John. "You're such a liar. Jesus Christ, John!"

His embarrassment turned to defensiveness. "Give me a break, Mag. Nobody likes getting old."

"The older we get," said Happy, "the less to look forward to and the more to regret."

Maggie folded her arms and grunted. "Fine, whatever, just put the right answer in and stop that alarm before I murder someone."

They added the numbers together again and this time Cheryl entered: **2-0-7**.

The car's alarm cut out.

The screen flashed with a green tick.

Silence.

Maggie removed her hands from her ears. "Oh, thank God!"

Leo was grinning. "We did it, guys. Nice!"

Cheryl looked at the clock. Just over eighty minutes left. Could they still do this? The fiasco over John's age might have already lost them time they couldn't afford. She really wanted to win.

Deposit on a flat. Deposit on a flat. You can do this.

A loud thud made everyone look up. The daylight above them disappeared as a sheet of metal slid across the entrance shaft. There was a loud *clunk* as it slotted into place.

John stared upwards. "What the hell was that? What is this?"

"Um, it's an escape room, boss," said Leo, "and I think we just finished part one."

"The plot does thicken," said Happy.

Cheryl wondered if what she was feeling was claustrophobia. With the daylight overhead, she hadn't felt quite so trapped. Even with the ladder gone, she'd still felt comforted by the sight of the sky. With it gone, she suddenly felt... buried. Movement caught her eye, and she turned back to the digital clock on the wall. The numbers were changing.

"What now?" said John, folding his arms and tapping his foot. All this was worrying him too — it was evident in his voice and body language. He was masking it with anger. "The clock is changing? Why?"

Leo shrugged. "Maybe we won more time."

"Or lost it," said Alfie.

"Just chill out, brethren." Monty was smirking. "You lot are a bunch of pussies."

The numbers settled, but on a far higher number than before. Happy stood in front of the display and read out the new figure. "One-hundred-and-sixty-seven-hours-and-fifty-eight seconds. What does that mean?"

Leo's eyes rolled in his head as he once again performed mental arithmetic. "It means the timer will end in... exactly one week. One-hundred-and-sixty-eight hours and counting."

Cheryl was impressed, even if the implications horrified her. "How d'you work that out so fast?"

He shrugged, blushing slightly. "Not that hard, really. The timer will end in exactly one week."

John was outraged. "Are they trying to suggest we'll be stuck down here for seven days? Not funny. They said a ninety minute maximum. I'll have their hides if it's a moment longer."

Monty grabbed John by the shoulder and rocked him. "Relax, boss. It's just to scare us, innit? Atmosphere and that. We ain't trapped. Course we ain't trapped."

Cheryl was breathing deeply, in-out-in-out-in-out. "Really?" she said. "Because it feels a lot like we're trapped. What do we do?"

Leo nudged her and smiled. She welcomed his playful touch, and it calmed her slightly. So did the relaxed tone of his voice. As tense as everyone was getting, Leo maintained his faith that all was fun and games. He pulled off his jacket and tossed it aside. "We're only stuck here as long it take us to escape, right? So let's escape. Onto the next round, am I right?"

Everyone looked at Leo, but it was unclear whether anyone agreed with his sentiments.

CHAPTER THREE

JOHN AND MAGGIE kept their distance as everyone searched for the next clue. Cheryl sensed the tension in the air and wondered if anybody else did too. Was she the only one worried? Leo could have been hurt by that falling ladder. What business would deign to leave its customers unsupervised?

She had to keep reminding herself that she was not a good judge in situations like this. New experiences were not her forte, so what she was experiencing might just be social anxiety. Admittedly, all she wanted to do was get back above ground and race home. Maybe, once she was out of this gloomy steel tunnel with the line of gently swinging lightbulbs, she would laugh at herself. Until then, she would remain unsettled.

The rooms branching off from each side of the straight main tunnel were barred like prison cells, with gaps too narrow to pass anything larger than an arm through. Only one of them was unlocked, and with no other discoveries they all congregated around it.

Monty took point. "Okay, guys. How you wanna do this?

Shall Monty take care of things, or should we all go in together?"

Cheryl imagined he thought referring to himself in the third-person was endearing or debonair, but it was neither of those two things in her opinion. "Maybe we should try working in teams of two," she suggested. "The rooms aren't that big. No point in bunching up."

"Okay," said Monty. "You're with me then, luv."

"Sounds good, *babe*!" She moved up beside Monty but stumbled when he bumped past her to get into the room. She wondered if he'd barged her on purpose. *Jerk.*

"What's in there?" Maggie called through the bars.

A metal table stood at the back of the room. Various containers were arranged on it. "I'm not sure," Cheryl shouted back. "Another puzzle, I think."

"Looks like a bar," said Monty, and he wasn't wrong. Cheryl's nose detected the bitter scent of alcohol, and one glass was clearly full of beer. Nestled between the various beverages was a red envelope which she picked up and opened. A piece of paper lay inside, and she slid it out. Before reading it, she turned to the others. "Shall I read it out loud?"

"Just get on with it," John said irritably. He was clearly still annoyed at the revelation of his age.

"Okay, okay! It says: *Take your tipple, youngest first.*"

"Another riddle," said Alfie, flopping against the other side of the bars and moaning. "Won't there be any skill games or something? This is boring, man."

"You're only saying that because you're dumb," said Monty.

"Your mum didn't think so last night!"

"My mum has a thing for retards."

"Shut up," said John. "Who knows the answer to the riddle? Anyone?"

"Hold on," said Cheryl. "Let me look at what we have. Maybe there are more clues to find."

Everyone remained silent while Cheryl examined the drinks on the table — six in total. She placed her hand around the beer glass and carefully lifted it. A foamy head fizzed on top, making her wonder how recently it had been poured. It wasn't warm in her hand, but nor was it cold.

"Hey," said Monty. "Hold it up. I think I just saw something." Cheryl raised the beer in the air and Monty leaned forwards. "Yeah," he said. "There's a letter written on the glass. Look!"

Cheryl turned the glass and, sure enough, there was a letter painted in white — with liquid eraser, maybe? It was a lowercase 'I.' She picked up another glass from the table and this one was a delicate, crystal flute. "I think this might be champagne," she guessed.

Maggie moaned outside the cell. "Oh, please, yes. Are there any rules about drinking it?"

Cheryl had an idea. She took the flute outside and handed it to Maggie in the tunnel. Maggie frowned, but took the flute as if it fit her hand perfectly. Cheryl saw a letter 'I' painted just above the stem.

"You want me to drink this?" Her lips wetted at the suggestion. "I could actually do with it right now. My head is killing me."

"I'm not sure," said Cheryl, "but the clue said to *take your tipple*. Champagne is your favourite?"

"Only because it costs a fortune," John muttered.

Maggie rolled her eyes. "Says the single malt drinker."

Cheryl turned back to Monty who was still standing inside the room. "Hey, Monty. I don't know what single malt is, but is there any on the table?"

"It's whiskey," said Monty, "and yeah, I think I have some here."

Cheryl retrieved a tumbler through the bars from Monty and handed it to John. She was taken aback by how 'woody' the drink smelled, and it made her slightly woozy. "Is this single malt?" she asked John.

John took the tumbler and put it to his mouth. He took a small sip and smacked his lips. "Yep, that's the good stuff."

"So how is this solving the riddle?" Leo was grinning, enjoying himself despite the tension. "Are we supposed to get tipsy?"

"There are six drinks," Cheryl explained. "Again, we need to leave me out because I haven't been factored into the games, but that's one drink for everyone. Maggie has champagne. John has single malt. What else do we have, Monty?"

"A beer and three other drinks. I think one might be cider."

"That's mine!" said Alfie. He retrieved the drink from Monty and held it up like he was relaxing at the club. "It's my lucky drink. Can't tell you how many times I've pulled after a night on this."

Leo nodded his head. "Nice!"

"There's a vodka here, I think," said Monty, lifting a tumbler of clear liquid.

Leo put his hand up like he was in class. "Here."

Cheryl was smiling now, enthused that they were about to solve another puzzle. It assured her they were still just playing a game, and that everything was as it should be. As long as they were solving puzzles, they were doing what they had come here to do. "Okay, okay, so we have a beer too. Happy, do you drink beer?"

Happy pulled a face and rubbed his tummy. "Too gassy at my age. No, if I do have the odd drink it's a gin and tonic."

Alfie chuckled. "That's such an old person drink, man."

Happy raised an eyebrow at the young lad. "It's remarkably refreshing."

45

"There's a gin and tonic *here*, I think." Monty handed a glass through the bars and Happy took it. There was a slice of lemon in it. He sipped at it and then sighed with pleasure.

"Okay," said Cheryl, now looking at Monty. "The beer must be yours then."

Monty grunted. "No, it ain't. I don't drink."

Cheryl frowned. "Really?"

"I'm Muslim, innit?"

"Oh, yes, of course, sorry; but it makes no sense. Who does the beer belong to if not you? Damn, I thought I had it."

Leo patted her on the back. "Bad luck, Cher. I thought you had it too."

John grunted. "Okay, keep thinking everyone. I'm sure the answer is obvious."

There was silence for half-a-minute while everyone thought about it. Eventually Alfie cleared his throat. "Um, Monty *does* drink. He's blagging you, Cher. I've seen him down enough pints to know."

"Shut the fuck up, bruh. I'll mash you up!"

Alfie glared through the bars at Monty. "What you lying for, bruh? We all seen you drink bare amounts."

John nodded and so did Maggie. Apparently this was a well-known secret. Leo, too, seemed as if he knew. "Who cares, Monty? If you like a drink, fair play."

Monty marched out of the room and back into the tunnel. "It ain't even like that, man. Me and a few lads from mosque might like a cheeky beer now and then, but it's serious fucking business. My old man finds out and he'll drown me in the canal. No one can *ever* find out, you get me?"

Leo held his hands up in a peaceful gesture. "Your life, Monty. I won't say a word to anyone."

Monty turned his glare on Cheryl. It was a hard, unfriendly look, and caused her to hold her hands up in surrender as well. "Who the heck am I going to tell, Monty? I barely know you."

He seemed to relax. "I'm a good Muslim, yeah? I just think some of the rules are…"

"Bullshit?" Leo suggested.

"Don't be saying shit about my faith, bruh."

"Ha! Make your mind up, dude. Look, chill out, we can all believe what we want to believe. Long as we're all good to one another, right?"

Monty nodded, although he glared at Leo a moment longer before finally looking away. "Nuff said about it, yeah?"

"Okay," said Cheryl, attempting to get things back on track. She hadn't forgotten about the prize money — or the time limit. "So, Monty, I know it's a touchy subject, but for the purposes of this game, can you pick up the beer, please?"

Monty retrieved the pint and brought it out. He appeared less angry now and more apprehensive, but rather than keep his feelings to himself, he shared them. "I trust all of you, yeah, but how did the jokers running this thing find out? You been spilling shit about us all, John?"

John sipped the single malt and sighed. "I said nothing to no one. I honestly don't know how they found out what we like to drink, but you can ask them about it once we get out of here. I shall be."

"This is getting personal," said Alfie after taking a long swig of his cider. "It ain't just a game, they're basing the puzzles on our lives. That's well iffy."

"It's in bad taste, I agree," said Happy, "but they probably didn't realise they would be prodding at open wounds. Most people aren't embarrassed by their age or what they drink."

"Right," said Leo. "I have nothing to hide. They can try to get inside my head all they want."

"I agree with Happy," said Maggie, arms folded and

mouth pursed. "How could the event organiser know that John would lie about his age?"

"Or that Monty don't want people to know he drinks," added Alfie.

The comments aggravated both men, so Happy put a hand up to prevent further comments. "Cheryl has this puzzle in the bag, so let's get back to her theory. We each have the right drink, so what next?"

"The letters," she said, having already thought through the next step. "Everyone has a letter on their glass, right?"

Everyone checked and discovered it to be true.

Alfie shrugged. "I have a 'G.' What does that stand for?"

Leo scratched a thumbnail over the letter on his vodka glass. "I have a 'U.' Reckon we have to spell out a word?"

John examined the letter on his glass. "That must be it. What order should we be in?"

"By age," said Cheryl. "*Take your tipple, youngest first.* Everyone needs to stand in a line, youngest to oldest." Everyone shuffled around until they had a line starting with Alfie and ending with Happy. "Great! Now read out your letters in order."

Alfie started. "G."

Leo. "U."

Monty. "I."

Maggie. "L."

John. "T."

Happy read out the letter on his gin and tonic. "Y."

Cheryl flicked her tongue back and forth while she put the letters together in her head. "G-U-I-L-T-Y. The letters spell *guilty*."

Leo stopped smiling. "Well, that's unsettling. What does it mean?"

Cheryl suddenly wished she had a drink in her hand. "I guess we'll find out."

"It's just a game," said Monty. "They're messing with us."

Cheryl had been chewing her lip but stopped now to speak. "I'm a little freaked out."

"I second that," said Maggie. She had taken her wooly hat off now and her dark hair fell in a ponytail over her shoulder. "All this drama is making me ill. I want to go to the hotel."

Happy told everyone to calm down. "Monty's right," he said. "This is all part of the experience. Being made to feel uncomfortable is what we expected, correct? People today demand shock value, they want to be frightened out of their skin, and the only way entertainment companies can get ahead is to push the envelope. We're getting our money's worth, that's all. I, for one, am having fun."

"You sound so certain," said Cheryl, wanting to be comforted by his words but not quite there yet. "You really think this is all okay?"

"Better to look on the bright side until left with no other choice, don't you agree? We came here to solve puzzles and, so far, I believe we've been doing that rather well. You most of all, Cheryl. You've impressed us all."

"It's true," said John, nodding earnestly.

Leo gave Cheryl a pat on the arm. "You've solved every puzzle so far. Now we have to find out what to do with the word *guilty*, so come on, genius, what's next?"

Suddenly everyone was looking at her, and she found it ironic that she had gained her colleague's respect through a game rather than work. "Maybe it'll allow us to open another room," she said, looking up the tunnel at the numerous barred gates. It was starting to resemble a prison landing and the subtle movements of the hanging lightbulbs made shadows twitch and flinch on the walls.

"We should check the locks," said Alfie. "See if any of them have opened."

"Good plan," said John. "Get to work."

One by one, they checked the other padlocks on the gates, and after a moment's searching Happy called out. "I think I have something here."

Cheryl was still feeling anxious, so she took off towards him like a firework, eager to begin a new puzzle. It kept her mind occupied.

"Letters," Happy explained once she reached him. "This padlock has six rollers, but there are letters instead of numbers. Perhaps we can spell out the word that was written on our glasses."

John barged his way to the front. "What are you waiting for then? Try the combination."

Happy nodded. His hands were calloused and his fingers gnarled, but he thumbed at the rollers gamely. Letter by letter, he spelled out the word GUILTY.

The padlock popped open with an audible *clack*.

"We're getting pretty good at this," said Leo, pressing up against Cheryl's hip. Was he touching her on purpose? "Maybe we're not all going to die down here after all."

"Not amusing," said John with a scowl.

"Yeah," said Cheryl, moving aside to open up some space between them. "Please don't say things like that."

"Sorry."

Happy yanked the cell door and it made the typical horror movie sound of 'rusty gate opening.' It set Cheryl's nerves on edge. Why was she so jumpy? Everyone here was a little para-noid, admittedly, but their rational selves were winning over — even if only barely. She, on the other hand, felt more and more like freaking out. She kept telling herself it was just the excitement of being in a social situation outside of work, but she felt like she was standing on a beach watching people swim shark-infested waters. She was the only one who could perceive the danger while everyone else flapped about blindly. Desperately, she wanted someone to freak out so that she could join them. She just couldn't be the first.

They didn't have to enter the unlocked cell to see what was inside for it was well lit. A large pallet of tiles took up most of the space. Maggie rubbed at her chin thoughtfully when she noticed them, and seemed troubled by something, but the tiles were unremarkable as far as Cheryl could tell.

"Those are Spanish Flag," said John, gripping the bars while he peered inside.

"Yeah," said Alfie. "We used to shift a tonne of those back when I first started with the company. What happened to them?"

John shrugged. "We were only making twenty-percent margin, so we changed suppliers. Alscon grew, we demanded better rates elsewhere."

Monty smirked. "Plus, I sold all the stock of Spanish Flag the supplier had to the Council when they refurbed the town college. They covered half-an-acre in this ugly stuff. Was a massive deal."

Maggie stopped staring at the tiles and looked at Monty. "Yeah, I remember. I had to go through a dozen different departments before someone at the town hall finally paid the bill. I remember it well because it was right around the time..." She trailed off, glancing at Happy for a split-second, then staring down at the floor. She cleared her throat. "I just remember it."

Cheryl was confused. "What? Right around the time of what?"

Happy put a hand on Cheryl's shoulder. "It was right around the time my niece disappeared. Her name was Polly, and she worked in sales."

"At Alscon?"

"Yes. I talked John into giving her a go. He'd just hired his nephew, Alfie, so I thought hiring my niece would make things fair and square."

John chuckled. "Polly was a good salesperson. Even gave Monty a run for his money."

"Beginner's luck," said Monty, but meant it lightheartedly. "Polly was a sweetheart. Wish I knew what happened to her."

"Yeah," said Alfie, staring glumly at the floor. "Me too."

Cheryl kept her focus on Happy who seemed at once cheerful and sad as he spoke about his missing niece. She felt bad asking for details, but it was hard to believe without knowing more. "Your niece just *disappeared?*"

He nodded. "It was after Alscon's year-end party. We were all staying overnight at this big country manor, the Claybrook Estate. Everyone was drinking too much, and having a good time, but Polly was gone when we prepared to leave the next morning. The police were involved; thought she might have gone for a walk around the grounds and gotten hurt or..." he shrugged, "*taken.* A search team went out. Rewards were offered. My sister even begged for Polly's safe return on the evening news, but no one ever found a single clue of her whereabouts. It was like she never existed. Except for the fact I miss her every day." He tapped the badge on his lapel. NEVER GIVE UP. "That's why I wear this every now and then, to remind myself to keep hope that one day the truth will come out. My sister deserves closure."

Cheryl's stomach turned. "That's horrible. I'm so sorry, Happy."

"We all are," said John. "Polly had a bright future. Probably would've been running Alscon by now. I could have retired to Spain."

Happy waved a hand at them. "Let's not reopen old wounds. It was two years ago. Two years next month in fact."

Monty shook his head and tutted. "Has it really been that long?"

"Yes, it has really been that long. Although it still feels like yesterday sometimes."

Alfie cleared his throat and nodded at the pallet of tiles. "So what's with these then? Why have they dumped a load of our old stock down here? How did they even get it?"

"It's *missing* stock," said Maggie. "Took me a moment to figure it out, but pallets 6–18 went missing before they ever made it to the construction site. Caused me a right headache at the time. Much like the one I have now."

Cheryl saw the orange '**6**' scrawled on the pallet's middle beam and realised what Maggie was saying. "You're telling me this pallet was stolen two years ago? And now it's here?"

"That's *exactly* what I'm telling you!" Maggie looked in pain, like every word out of her mouth sent sparks through her brain. "We mark our pallets with a fluorescent orange marker. This pallet is one of ours. Stolen."

Alfie loosened his scarf and rubbed his neck. "I'm telling you, man, this is personal. This company knows our ages, our drinking habits, and now this... Not to mention the fact they have the front half of Monty's old motor down here."

Leo flinched. "What?"

"That TVR," said Alfie. He sounded a little hysterical and continued loosening his shirt like he was overheating, despite the chill in the air. "That's Monty's TVR. He wrote the stupid thing off less than a month after he got it."

"I knew I recognised it," said Leo, his face suddenly lighting up. He pointed at Monty. "You must have had that thing for all of two weeks. I figured you swapped it for the Range Rover. Wow, I can't believe I didn't recognise it right away."

Monty couldn't look anyone in the eye. In fact, he turned his back on them as he spoke. "Thing was a death trap. They

53

shouldn't be allowed to sell 'em. Anyway, that's not my old car, it's just the same model. They probably got one at the scrap yard just to mess with me."

"That's what *I* thought at first," said Alfie, "but not no more. I reckon it's the exact same one, bruh."

"It's a coincidence," Monty repeated.

"You did write it off though?" asked Leo. He looked towards the sports car, rear half still missing.

Monty shrugged, still not looking at them. "Don't really remember what happened, but I must have ended up in a spin or something. Tore the back half away but, somehow, I didn't get a scratch on me. I'm lucky to be alive, bruh, I swear down. You'll never catch me in a sports car again. Luxury SUVs all the way for Monty Rizwan."

Leo swallowed a lump in his throat, a bulge rolling down his long neck. "How could they know about the accident? How could they have known you lost the back half? Do they have your insurance records or something?"

Monty shrugged ignorance. "If it's a joke, I ain't laffin."

Alfie rubbed at his stunted hand as if it was hurting him. It was rare he did anything to bring attention to his deformity, which was why it made him appear so vulnerable. "These people are screwing with us," he said. "I'm telling you. We should have kept our phones. We need help."

There was a chill in the air that everyone seemed to notice at once. They were all wearing coats, but they hugged themselves and moved closer together. Cheryl could still feel heat being blasted from the slim vents at ankle-height, but she had the suspicion the temperature had been turned down. The fans overhead rotated sluggishly.

"This isn't a game," said Maggie. "No one is having fun here."

Cheryl hugged herself and shuddered as a chill ran along her shoulders. "So, what are you saying?"

Maggie shook her head. She didn't have an answer.

Leo moved in front of John. "Who is this company, boss? What are they playing at?"

"Yeah," said Alfie. "I'd like to know too."

John stared at the floor and didn't look up for several moments. "They've taken things too far. They probably just researched us to make the games more engaging, but I don't care. They won't be getting any of our business, I promise you. Any more of this and they'll end up in court."

That wasn't the question Leo had asked, so Cheryl asked it again. "*Who* are they, John? What is the company called?"

John squinted as though trying to remember. "They were called, um, yeah, I remember, they were called *Retribution Ltd*."

"Yes," said Happy. "That was the name."

"Wow!" said Leo. "Nothing worrying about that at all. *Retribution*? Seriously? And the word *guilty* written on our glasses. Is the company run by some guy called Judge McPunisher?"

Monty tutted. "Come on, you lot, keep your marbles. It's just a game, innit? Fair play to this *Retribution Ltd* for taking their shit seriously. They don't mess around, and I like it. I might even invest in their operation. Been meaning to make my money work harder for me."

Maggie unfolded her arms and rubbed at her forehead. "I don't believe you, Monty. You're pretending you aren't as freaked out as the rest of us, but it's bullshit."

"Nobody's hurt, are they? If somebody wanted to get us, why go to this length or expense? There are easier ways to mess somebody up, you get me? The only reason to spend money is to make money, so this is obviously a business. A business that won't get our cash if we're injured, so just chill, woman."

Maggie nodded and seemed to relax. In fact, everybody

did for it was true. Why would anybody go to such expense merely to screw with a group of office workers? This was all part of an experience, and *Retribution Ltd* was doing its best to win a corporate account.

Despite the relief, Cheryl felt like throwing up. She hadn't worked with these people long enough to trust them, and part of her mind nagged her to get the hell out of that hole. She never should have gone down there.

What if Alscon has drawn the anger of some deranged madman and this is his maniacal revenge? Mum will kill me if I get murdered and chopped up.

"I think we should just carry on playing," said Leo. "It's the only way we'll get answers. There's a pallet of stolen tiles in that cell so why don't we think about what that means?"

"It means," said John. "That one of you is a fucking thief. And God help them if I find out who."

"Hey, um, guys?" Leo was crouched behind the pallet of tiles, and he looked at them over the top now. It was obvious from his expression that he'd found something.

"What is it?" Cheryl accidentally yelled the question and embarrassed herself. Her nerves remained unsettled, and she desperately wished she still had her phone so she could call her mother — even if it was only to hear a lecture. *I warned you not to go, Cher, but you never listen.* Then she would call the police and tell them she was trapped in a gloomy, steel tunnel fifteen feet underground.

But hey, at least I'm out of the house. Yay for me.

Leo reached down and produced another tablet like the one that was affixed to the TVR's engine. He placed it on top of the tiles with the screen facing everybody. "You think this might give us answers?"

"Does it switch on?" asked John. He stood close to Maggie now, the previous distance between them non-existent. His jaw was clenched and his hands locked into fists — like he was just begging for somebody to shout at. God help anyone at *Retribution Ltd.*

"Hold on, let me try." Leo prodded a button at the bottom of the tablet and the screen came immediately to life. A video started playing.

There was nothing on screen except for a man; but it was no ordinary man. This person had no eyes — only flat, bumpy flesh over hollow sockets. His nose and mouth were normal, but his head lacked a single hair. Nor did he have eyebrows or facial hair. He was more mannequin than man. "To lie is to be human," he said in a rasping hiss like crushed insects, "but to steal is a crime. All of you are deceivers, all of you are liars, but only one of you is a thief. Will that person come forward and confess?"

Cheryl looked at the others, but no one moved a muscle. They stood, transfixed by the abomination on screen.

The eyeless man sighed and ran a slender set of fingers over the patchy skin covering his eye sockets. "I see you not, but I am certain none of you has stepped forwards. As you wish; in lieu of dignity, the thief shall be coerced to confess. Punishment shall be dispensed."

Leo shifted uncomfortably. "What does that mean?"

Cheryl shushed him.

The horrific stranger continued, thin lips barely moving as he spoke. "The room beside this one is locked with an automatic bolt. Inside, are enough supplies to help you survive one week. In seven days, an anonymous call to the police shall see you set free, but without the supplies in the next room, you shall be long dead by the time help arrives."

"I fucking told you," said Alfie. "We're screwed. This is fucked! Fucked!"

Maggie wailed. John had to place an arm around her waist to keep her in place. She buried her head against his chest and sobbed.

Cheryl teetered and feared she might fall. Was this a joke? Because it wasn't funny. She moved next to Leo, not touching him, but close enough to grab him if the need arose.

The stranger kept on, giving them no time to digest what they were hearing. He whispered now, his voice like running salt. "If you wish to unlock the next room, the thief must reveal themselves and accept punishment. A man who takes with one hand must lose the other. That is the price to be paid. One hand will secure the lives of all of you."

The tablet faded to black. Leo jabbed at the button but nothing happened. "There must've been some kind of code or script or—" He shook his head as though forcing himself not to get carried away. "Yeah, well, whatever it was, it must have fired when I pressed the button. The tablet's dead."

Maggie clutched John like he was holding her afloat. "There must be a way to get it back on. We can email the police. Make it come back on, Leo. This is getting out of hand."

Leo picked the tablet up and thrust it at her. "Give it a shot, Mag! I'm telling you, it's dead."

Maggie didn't take the tablet. Her bottom lip trembled, and she looked away. John thrust out his palm. "All right, Leo, rein it in. You're acting the twat."

Leo folded his arms and swore under his breath. Offended, he muttered, "Watch who you're calling a twat."

"This is insane," said Cheryl, fearing she was going to puke. Her tummy felt like the static on an old-fashioned television. "Who did you... who did you guys piss off?"

John glared at her. "No one! I have no idea why this is happening. It's a bloody outrage."

Monty pointed a finger at Happy. "You said you checked this company out, Hap, and that it was legit. What the hell?"

Happy looked like he might burst into tears. "I-I don't know what to tell you. I'm so sorry."

John was growling. "It's not your fault, Hap. They'll pay for this, trust me. We've been brought down here under false pretences."

Monty smashed his fist into his palm. "Who do they think they're messing with? I'll sue their arses off. My uncle's a solicitor, innit?"

John patted Monty on the back in support of his statement. "I'm with you, dude. They picked on the wrong group of people. If this is about money or blackmail, they won't get any joy from us."

Cheryl took a deep breath and held it to ensure she didn't throw up. "You keep saying *they*, but what if it's just one guy? The guy without any eyes, maybe he's a maniac."

"One man couldn't do all this," said Monty, "and you think we wouldn't remember pissing off a guy with no eyes in his head?"

Leo shrugged. "I've dated worse."

Alfie sat on the pallet of tiles and shook his head in despair. "Whatever the reason, we're trapped down here. Part of me is still hoping it's a game, but if what that guy on the tablet said is true, we might need to get through an entire week down here. Who's this thief he was on about? Is there any truth to it?"

Maggie wiped tears from her eyes but seemed angry now rather than afraid. She still seemed ill, however. "Somebody here is responsible for these tiles disappearing off one of our lorries, that much is obvious. So, come on! Who is it?"

Silence. Nobody moved a muscle, probably for fear it would implicate them.

"There's no point hiding it," said Cheryl, trying to keep

her tone friendly rather than adversarial. "Let's just do what we have to do to get out of here."

Monty turned on her, poking a finger in her face. "How do we know the thief ain't you, luv?"

"Um, because I wasn't even with the company until three months ago. Oh, and I'm not even supposed to be here. Whatever grudge this psychopath has is against the six of you, not me. I'm an innocent bystander."

"She's right," said Leo. "Out of all of us here, Cheryl is the only one we know is innocent."

"You're here because of me, Cher." Maggie's bottom lip quivered as she spoke. "I'm so sorry."

Too right, thought Cheryl. She should beat the woman's head in, but what would it help? "You couldn't have known, Mag." To make it clear, she gave the woman a hug. "I'm not interested in blame. We just need to get through... whatever this is."

Maggie seemed to appreciate the hug, and she tried smiling, but when it turned to more tears, she buried her head back in John's chest. He rubbed at her back absentmindedly. He'd grown red in the cheeks, and his jaw flexed like it had a pulse running through it. Eventually words exploded from his mouth. "Just come out with it! One of you is a dirty thief, and I demand to know who it is. I gave you all jobs and this is how you repay me? *Alscon* took a write-down for those tiles. That's money out of my own pocket. Whoever's guilty, I want you to look me in the eye right now and admit it."

No one came forward.

John swore at them and stormed off, leaving Maggie floundering as her security blanket removed itself, but there was nowhere for John to go. He was forced to stop only a few feet from the group and ended up spinning back around to face them again. This time, however, he wasn't angry. He was visibly concerned. "I smell gas!"

Leo paced towards him. "What? From where?"

Both men peered into the nearest room off the side of the tunnel. Leo pointed. "Shit! It's coming from in there. Those are the supplies we need."

Everyone raced to join them. Cheryl grabbed the gate and stared through the bars. Inside were several plastic crates of water, several of milk, and boxes upon boxes of crackers. Not a diet fit for a king, but enough to keep them alive for a week if they were truly trapped down there.

This still has to be a joke, right? This is part of the game. To scare us?

The smell of gas wafted through the bars and at the back of the cell a small flame suddenly burst to life. It rose out of what looked like a Bunsen Burner — a slim copper shaft like the ones Cheryl used to use at school.

The blue flame rose higher and higher towards a thin cotton scarf decorated with pink hearts hanging two-feet above it. The fabric glistened, soaked through with what could only be petrol — Cheryl's nose told her so. She also noticed a red plastic canister hanging from the ceiling. The wet scarf had been knotted around and stuffed into its spout. She'd once read that petrol exploding like a bomb was a Hollywood invention, but she didn't want to find out.

"The flame's going to ignite that scarf," said Leo, putting words to Cheryl's thoughts. "It's rigged to burn all the supplies!"

She nodded. "And maybe us."

Alfie was staring up at the scarf as well, his eyes wide and terrified. It looked like he wanted to say something but was unable.

The flame rose higher.

They had minutes. Maybe less.

"How do we put it out?" Maggie had her mittened hands over her mouth like a frightened child. "What do we do?"

"The thief needs to own up," said John. "Right now."

Leo kicked the bars, making them rattle. "Come on, man. Own up."

"*You* own up!" Alfie pointed a finger. "It was probably you, anyway. Jealous of the money we make in sales."

"It wasn't me, Alfie, trust me."

John's anger was rising like the flame inside the cell. "Somebody own up right now or I'll sack the lot of you."

Happy moved towards John. "Calm down."

John shoved him aside. "*You* calm down."

"This is bullshit, man." Monty shook his head and started walking away down the tunnel. Leo followed, but when he reached out to grab the salesman's arm, Monty lashed out and shoved him back. "Keep your hands off me, bruh, or I'll mash you up."

Leo kept his hands away. "Sorry, but you can't just walk away from this, Monty. If this turns out not to be a joke then we'll starve down here if we lose those supplies. You want to take that risk?"

"I don't give a shit, bruh!"

Leo stared at Monty with an expression that seemed to communicate something between them. "I don't think that dude on the tablet was messing around. Unless the thief owns up, our only chance of survival is about to go up in flames. We *have* to play ball."

Monty shouldered Leo aside and tried to walk away again, but it was like watching a rat trapped in a maze. Monty kept pacing back and forth, but there was nowhere for him to go except one end of the tunnel or the other.

"We don't have long left," said Cheryl, hands trembling on the bars as she watched the supplies about to go up in flames. "Please, whoever stole the stupid tiles, just own up. Please!"

Leo stood in Monty's path. "Dude, if this is for real, we're going to starve to death. Or maybe even burn."

Monty shoved Leo again, but this time Leo held his ground and frustrated him. "Get out my way, bruh. I'm not messing around. This *gandu* wants to mess with me, bring it on. He ain't got nothing on me."

"You sure? Because those tiles got here somehow."

"Why the fuck would I need to steal when I'm already minted? Get real, bruh, yeah? I'll mash you up if you don't get out my face. So move! Come on, man, don't make me drop you." Monty bunched his fists. He was breathing heavily, and almost trembling with frustration, but Leo would not move out of his way. "What is your problem, bruh? I didn't steal no goddamn tiles, so just move out the way. How would I even get away with it? They investigated at the time, innit? There's no proof. Leo, I swear, man, just move. I didn't do it. Move!"

Cheryl saw John move away from the bars. There was a look of shock on his face. "Monty? I don't believe it. It was you, wasn't it?"

Monty sneered. "I ain't no fucking thief, John. You know me."

"Yeah, I do, which is why I know you're lying. You're panicking. You actually stole the tiles. Tell me why."

Monty's mouth moved as if words were trying to escape. He resisted them for a while, but then couldn't help himself and ended up yelling. "You made a fortune on that council deal, John, and you gave me, what, three-grand as a bonus?"

John shook his head, eyes wide and disbelieving. "You earn a higher salary than I do for Christ's sake! You must think I'm made of money, but I only get paid when the company does well. *You* get paid regardless. So yes, sometimes your hard work pays off for me, Monty, but when sales are bad, it's me that suffers, not you. Welcome to the real world. You don't like it, start your own goddamn business. I've treated you more than fairly."

Alfie frowned at Leo suspiciously. "You knew, didn't you?

You were hounding Monty because you knew he was the thief. How?"

Leo sighed and lifted his chin as if he suddenly found it hard to meet anyone's gaze. "I had no proof, but I suspected Monty was behind the missing tiles, yeah. He signed the purchase orders when they came through from the council, which was weird. Usually he would rather do anything other than paperwork. Everyone at the office is forever doing his admin, but he gets a pass because he's the company's top salesperson. I get it, and I don't mind, but on this occasion he was adamant about doing all the paperwork himself. I figured he wanted to make sure nothing got screwed up — it was the biggest deal Alscon had ever had up until that point — but after twelve-grand's worth of tiles went missing, I wondered."

"Why didn't you say something," John demanded. He looked ready to keel over. A boss probably expected a certain amount of employee disloyalty, but he appeared to be taking this betrayal hard. Cheryl felt bad for him.

"I kept quiet because I didn't want to stir a cauldron full of shit on the back of a hunch. Monty's untouchable. I figured I'd be the one to come off worse if I said anything."

"I would've believed you, Leo," said Maggie, rubbing at her throat as if it were sore. "Monty has always been out for number one."

Monty hissed at her. "Takes one to know one, plastic Sally."

"Fuck you, Monty. You're just a thief."

"Hey!" Cheryl hollered at them from over by the bars. She still couldn't take her eyes off the growing flame. "Monty is the thief, he's admitted it, so come on, we need to deal with the problem at hand. We have to rescue these supplies."

"Yeah, yeah, okay." Leo nodded. "What do we do, Cher?"

"I... Shit, I don't know."

"Admit you're the thief, Monty." Happy had been standing

idly to one side while the rest of them had been arguing, but he re-engaged now. "Say it out loud so that anyone who might be listening will hear you."

Monty pulled a face. "Fuck's sake. Fine! My name is Monty Rizwan, and I stole a bunch of shitty tiles from Alscon. Fucking sue me!"

"I'll do more than that," said John, taking off his coat and throwing it down.

There was a sharp *click* and a gate sprung open. It was the one *opposite* the cell with the supplies. Cheryl groaned. "No, the wrong gate opened! We need those supplies."

John rolled up his shirt sleeves, and looked like he might attack Monty, but instead he hurried into the newly opened cell. He returned ten seconds later holding two items — a sharp-looking meat cleaver and a small water pistol with a funnel attached to the top. Nothing about his expression suggested he knew what they were for.

"What the hell?" Maggie clutched her forehead and grimaced. The shadows beneath her eyes had grown worse, and she was sweating profusely. "I can't take much more of this. What are we supposed to do with those?"

"We take Monty's hand," said Leo grimly. "The dude on the tablet said the man who takes with one hand must lose the other."

"Fuck that shit," said Monty, backing away.

Alfie frowned. "What about the water pistol?"

Cheryl didn't know what disturbed her more; what she was thinking or the fact she arrived at the conclusion before anybody else. "That's how we put out the flame. We need to fill it with blood."

John stared at the cleaver in his hand, then started towards Monty.

CHAPTER FOUR

"GET the fuck away from me, bruh. What you gonna do, hack me to pieces, yeah?"

John didn't seem like he knew what he intended, but he clearly planned on doing *something*. His eyes glistened with hurt and anger as he waved the meat cleaver at Monty. "There's no other option."

"Stay back or I'll drop you, John. I ain't messing around."

What Cheryl found difficult to believe was that nobody else moved. They just stood there and watched while their boss stalked their colleague with a meat cleaver. Behind her, the flame continued rising, just six-inches from the dangling scarf now. The petrol canister would soon ignite and destroy the supplies. "We have to think of a way around this," she yelled at the others. "Think!"

"We know how to put the fire out," said Alfie, pale as a bed sheet. "Monty needs to lose a hand so we can squirt his blood through the bars."

"I'm sorry," said John, still stalking Monty. "If I don't do this, everybody dies."

Monty seemed to realise he was about to get hacked up by

a meat cleaver, and his coffee-coloured skin grew pale. "Are you crazy? Boss, t-think about what you're doing. If this turns out to be a game..."

"Then I'll blame *Retribution Ltd* for putting me in this situation." He spoke without a hint of emotion and it made Cheryl shudder. Surely he wasn't about to go through with this? It was a joke.

Monty looked left and right, searching for solutions to his dilemma. "Take Alfie's hand! Yeah, it's fucking useless anyway."

Alfie slipped his deformed hand under his scarf, embarrassed by it, but then his face contorted into an angry scowl. "You're the one that's useless, you thieving prick!"

"This isn't a game," said Leo, pacing back and forth and shaking his head. "This is past the point any sane person would go to have fun. Someone is playing with our lives. This is actually happening."

"Is it?" Happy stared at him. "I mean, are we sure this isn't just part of a game designed to scare us? Have you jumped to ghoulish conclusions? We should stop and think."

"That meat cleaver doesn't look like a prop to me," said Alfie. "It's real."

Monty backed up to where the ladder had been, his safety running out. His heel struck a piece of steel rung still lying on the ground and he yelped in fright. "C-Come on, John. Stop this. Please, stop it."

John lifted the cleaver, his expression impassive. "You brought this on yourself, Monty. I don't want to do it, but I have no choice. If you volunteer, we can do it quick and easy."

"You can't cut someone's hand off quick and easy," said Cheryl, stomach acid rising into her throat.

Happy was shaking his head. "Take a second, John. Think this through. Don't do anything you can't undo."

John glanced back and seemed to hesitate, possibly

coming to his senses, but before he had a chance to rethink, Monty rushed him, ducking down and picking up a discarded steel rung. He brought it up and around, and whacked his boss right in the side of the head. John staggered sideways into the wall, dropping the cleaver and water pistol as he put both hands against the side of his head.

Cheryl cried out, but she remained rooted to the spot — forced to watch.

With madness and fear in his eyes, Monty retrieved the fallen meat cleaver and then grabbed John by his wrist. Still dazed from the blow to the head, John offered no resistance, even as Monty yanked his hand out in front of him with the palm facing upwards.

Happy cried out for him to stop.

Leo sprinted as fast as he could. "Monty, don't!"

Monty slashed the cleaver through the air.

Thunk!

John collapsed backwards into a heap on the ground. He didn't cry out in pain, only panted like he was out of breath. His eyes were wide and disbelieving.

Cheryl doubled over and vomited, sickened by the sound alone — soft meat being brutalised. Despite her horror though, she couldn't help but glance over at the result of what had just happened.

John's hand had not completely come away from the wrist. It hung by a loose bundle of nerves and sinewy blood vessels. Blood spurted into the air, covering Monty who stood staring at the bloody cleaver in his hand like he couldn't believe what he'd just done. He slumped against the container's wall and stared at John on the ground. "I-I'm sorry. Boss, I'm so sorry."

Cheryl vomited again, bile stinging the back of her throat. Happy turned away and wept. Maggie became a statue, sickly pale except for the darkness beneath her eyes. Only Alfie and

Leo were in control enough to try to help John. Leo propped him up while Alfie grabbed his bleeding wrist and held it aloft. Cheryl remembered their First Aid certificates hanging on the cafeteria wall at the office and felt a pang of hope that they would know what to do.

"We have to stop the bleeding," said Alfie. "Shit, what do we do?"

Leo was trembling, already spattered in John's blood. "W-We need to make a tourniquet."

"I'm sorry," Monty murmured. "So sorry."

"Just back up," Alfie shouted at him. "What the hell, man?"

Cheryl wanted to carry on puking, but she couldn't stand by while someone bled to death. She hurried over and yanked at Alfie's scarf. "Take it off," she said. "Take it off and use it to wrap his wrist."

Alfie looked at her for a second like he didn't understand, but then he nodded and began unravelling his scarf. He pulled it free and went to wrap it around John's wrist, but then paused and went for the water pistol instead. It had been lying on the ground nearby.

Cheryl frowned. "What are you doing? You need to help John."

Alfie propped the funnel of the water pistol beneath John's gushing wrist, catching the thick, cascading blood. "We need to put out the fire."

"We need to stop John from bleeding to death!" Cheryl snatched at the scarf. "You're sick!"

Leo grabbed her arm and stared at her with his deep brown eyes that were nothing except serious. "Alfie's right. Give him two-seconds."

"Two-seconds and John might die."

John moaned. "D-Do it. It's... okay."

Cheryl looked at John and then at Leo. She hated herself for it, but she nodded. "Do it quickly."

Alfie positioned the funnel beneath John's bleeding stump and it filled up fast. The chamber inside the water pistol darkened even as blood spilled everywhere. It was warm, which somehow made it worse. Cheryl had to put a hand against her mouth to keep from gagging. John's eyes fluttered like he was having a dream, except he was awake.

"Hurry," said Happy from over by the bars. "You need to hurry."

Alfie's hands were shaking. The pistol's chamber was half-full. John had no more time.

"Go," Cheryl urged. "Alfie, that's enough."

Alfie leapt up with the blood-filled water pistol and raced towards the supplies. Cheryl watched him over her shoulder, wondering if he would be able to put out the fire in time to—

Light exploded, searing her eyes.

A monstrous boom obliterated her hearing.

Hot air blanketed Cheryl from head to toe and she saw Happy and Alfie's silhouettes knocked from their feet and flying backwards through the air. The lights overhead swung back and forth wildly causing Shadows to dance over everything.

Then Cheryl's head filled with screams.

Cheryl screamed along with everybody else, although the noise came out distorted. Sound took on a tinny quality and her vision blurred. The heat in the tunnel faded quickly, but it was still enough to make her sweat.

She realised she was lying on her side.

Mum. I want mum.

Leo appeared at the edge of her swirling vision and he

grabbed her. He shouted but his words were garbled. Too bewildered to understand, she turned her focus to John lying next to her. Her boss still lived. His bulging eyes darted in every direction. His wrist still spurted blood. He might have been crying out in pain. She couldn't be sure.

Too confused.

She felt something wet, realised John was bleeding on her.

More movement alerted her. Leo was offering his belt. She took the leather strap and retrieved Alfie's scarf, then secured both around John's wrist, pulling them as tight as she could get them. The bleeding slowed to a seeping trickle. John slumped back against the wall, breathing steadily. With Leo's help, she eased him into a sitting position against the wall and hoped he wouldn't die.

Please dad, don't be dead. Just wake up!

This can't be happening. I don't want to be here.

Leo was in her face again, mouthing words she couldn't understand. His dark brown eyes lit up every time the swaying bulbs overhead shone down on them. She felt safe in those eyes, and she dared not look away. But what was he trying to tell her?

Suddenly her ears popped. Sound came rushing back in cacophonous, horrific glory. Leo's words finally formed in her head and she realised he was asking if she was okay. For a moment, she could only stare at him in response. "W-What happened?"

"The petrol exploded."

Cheryl peered down the steel tunnel and saw billowing black smoke coming from one of the side rooms. Her eyes itched and she quickly had to look away. Alfie and Happy lay on the ground, unmoving. Maggie was on her hands and knees, spluttering and moaning. The only one standing was Monty, far enough away from the blast to remain a spectator. He was silent and staring.

Cheryl felt tears in her eyes and didn't know if the smoke had caused them. "W-We need to do something. Help! Somebody, please help us! HELP!"

Mum, help! Dad's fallen down.

Leo grabbed her and pulled her into an embrace. He spoke directly into her ear. "We have to put out the fire, Cher. The smoke alone is enough to kill us trapped down here."

"W-What about the others? They need help."

"There'll be no help for any of us if we suffocate. Come on!"

Leo released her and rushed to deal with the smoke. Cheryl got up and went after him so that they discovered the destruction together. She reached out and grabbed his hand almost without realising it.

The petrol canister still hung from the ceiling, but it was a blackened hunk of plastic now. The supplies were ablaze, but the flames were struggling for life. The plastic sheeting melted and curled in on itself, and only the wooden pallet at the bottom truly burned. The melting plastic, however, was the cause of the noxious black smoke.

"Some of the water is okay," said Leo, pointing to one of several large bottles still intact. "We need to get it away from the fire."

Cheryl moved back while Leo stepped inside the cell. He covered his mouth and nose with a forearm but coughed and spluttered anyway. He groped half-blind at the burning pallet, and several times he hissed as he burned himself, but he kept battling until he got his fingers beneath a blue plastic loop attached to the lid of one of the five-litre bottles of water. He yanked it, but the heated plastic wrapping had constricted around it. "Damn it, come on!"

Cheryl realised he needed help. She hurried forward and yanked at the edge of the plastic wrapping, trying to pull it free. It was hot and viscous, melting against the skin of her fingertips, but she ignored the pain and tugged even harder. They worked the bottle free together. It was heavy, and as Leo lifted it, it pulled him off balance. The flames licked at his forearm and caught on his shirtsleeve. He wheeled backwards out of the cell, dragging the water bottle with him, but also taking part of the fire. Frantically, he batted at the flame spreading along his forearm, but it was a losing battle. He was about to go up like Guy Fawkes.

He's going to burn right in front of me.

Cheryl yanked off her denim jacket and threw it over Leo's elbow, patting him down as quickly as she could.

The fire went out.

The panic drained from Leo's eyes, but he gritted his teeth in pain when she lifted her jacket away from his arm. The back of his hand was red and blistered. "I'm okay," he said, obviously seeing the concern on her face. "Just a little singed. We still need to deal with those flames." He nodded at the large bottle of water on the ground between them. It was better than a water pistol full of blood, and he quickly unscrewed the lid. With both arms, he then heaved the bottle upwards and upended it over the flaming pallet. The flames choked, generating more black smoke, but then Leo tilted the bottle even more and doused the melting plastic. The black smoke turned grey and white, then eventually gave off little more than a few wispy tendrils. The whole time, the spilled water turned to vapour with an angry *hiiiissssssssssss.*

Both Cheryl and Leo broke into coughing fits. They turned their back on the poisonous air and covered their mouths. "Christ on a bike," said Leo. "I think I just wrecked a lung."

"Are you okay? Your hand!"

"It's not as bad as it looks. We should help the others."

"Leo, this is really happening, isn't it?"

73

He stared at her for a moment as though he didn't know what to say, then hugged her tightly. "We'll get through this, Cher. I promise."

Happy let out a groan from the floor. Cheryl broke away from Leo to go and help the old office manager. She rolled him onto his back, and he blinked his eyes, staring up at the ceiling. His right cheek was swollen and beaded with blood. Otherwise he seemed okay. His thick, sheepskin coat probably acted like armour. The badge on his lapel caught the light. NEVER GIVE UP. "Ch-Cheryl? What happened?"

Cheryl took his wrinkled hand and held it. He was trembling. "The petrol ignited, but you're going to be okay, Happy."

"Is help coming?"

"I don't think so. We'll have to figure this out on our own."

Happy tried to sit up, but she pushed him back down. He started to panic. "Is-Is everyone okay?"

Cheryl looked at Alfie, still unmoving on the ground. "I don't know. Just take a second, okay?"

Leo shuffled over to check on Alfie, shaking the lad and calling his name. A tense moment ensued while they waited to see if he responded. Then, like a loaded spring, Alfie sat up, gagging and coughing and rubbing at the back of his head. His gelled hair was all over the place like a modern art sculpture. "Shitting 'ell, am I dead?"

"No," said Leo. "Nobody's dead, and it's going to stay that way. There's a way out of this and we'll find it."

Alfie clutched his head and moaned. A line of blood ran parallel to his left eyebrow and it looked like someone had taken a hammer to him. "I need a fag," he mumbled.

Maggie remained hunched on her hands and knees, still hacking and coughing. Cheryl crawled over and rubbed her on the back. "Mag? Maggie, are you okay?"

She looked at Cheryl blankly. "I want to go home. I want to go see my Andrew."

"I know you do, Mag. We all want to get out of here."

"I'm so sorry, Cheryl. I... I would never have brought you here if I'd known. I wouldn't have!"

"I know, Mag. It's not your fault."

Maggie shook her head, tears slicing streaks through the soot on her cheeks. "It is! I didn't want to be the only woman here. There never were any theatre tickets, Cher. I lied."

"What? Maggie, what are you saying?"

"Help! I need help here." It was Monty calling. He was crouched over John, slapping his injured boss on the cheek and trying to rouse him. "I think he's dead."

Cheryl rose on shaky legs and hurried over to John. She wished she'd chosen life as a nurse or doctor — not that she had the brains for it — because she suddenly found herself surrounded by injured people with no knowledge of how to help them.

John's eyes were closed and he was chalk-white, but not dead. She could see him breathing. "I think he's passed out from shock," she reassured Monty who looked utterly devastated. John's blood covered his hands and face. How the hell had this happened?

It's a bad dream. I must have eaten a dodgy Pot Noodle and now I'm tripping.

"I did this," Monty said. "I chopped his hand off."

Cheryl nodded. "Yeah, you did, but to be fair he was trying to do the same to you. It's done, either way. Let's just help each other as best we can, okay? Monty, do you hear me?"

"Is he going to be all right?"

"I don't know, Monty. Are *you* okay?"

He blinked and a tear ran down his cheek. He was nothing like the confident salesman she knew and mildly

75

despised. He was terrified. They all were. "I-I'm okay," he eventually told her, although he didn't look it. "Just tell me what to do."

Cheryl touched his shoulder softly. "Do nothing."

"I have what's left of the water." Leo called over to her. He was arranging the plastic bottles together in the tunnel's centre. He opened one up and helped Alfie take a swig. Then he used some to wipe Happy's burnt face.

Happy waved him off. "Don't fuss over me, boy. I'm fine."

"I don't want you to get an infection, dude."

"The least of my worries. Thank you, Leo, but I'm better left alone."

Alfie got to his feet, but immediately collapsed against the wall. He gagged and spat on the ground but got ahold of himself a moment later. "W-Why is this happening, man?"

"You tell me," said Cheryl. "I was tricked into being here, apparently." Maggie moaned at the comment, and attempted to apologise, but Cheryl spoke over her. "Somebody has one hell of a grudge against Alscon, that's for sure. One of you must know why. To do all this..." She waved an arm around the steel tomb they were in. "This wasn't done on a whim. Somebody planned this. Somebody wanted to punish you all. Why?"

Leo shook his head. "I honestly have no idea, Cher."

"Bullshit! You're not innocent, Leo. You can't be. We already found out Monty is a thief, so what will be the next secret revealed? Wouldn't you rather volunteer the information than have it used against you?"

He looked wounded. "I don't have any secrets, Cher, I promise."

"I've known Leo for several years," said Happy, making it stiffly up onto his feet. "He's a good lad. Obviously, there's a reason for all this, but let's not jump to conclusions, Cheryl. Not yet."

Cheryl glared at Leo, wanting him to be the sleazy, sexist asshole she suspected him to be, but what she saw was somebody else. Immature, Leo may be, but the concern on his face was real, and it was not just for himself. It was for her. "I'm sorry," she said. "Maybe this isn't your fault."

"It's okay, Cher. You were dragged into this by a bunch of people you've known for three months. I'd be pissed off too. Let's just find a way out of this hole, okay? We can figure out the rest later."

"All right, Leo, I trust you, but I need to take a moment, okay? This... this is all too much."

He smiled at her compassionately. "I have water and half-burned crackers, so how about you and I have lunch together later?"

Cheryl chuckled. "Sure, just don't get any ideas."

"You're safe with me, I promise."

She wished she could have believed him.

⸻

Everyone sat in a circle around John and for a while nobody spoke. They kept a silent vigil, drinking water and chewing partially singed crackers, but the vigil was really for themselves. None of them knew if they would ever get out of there. Cheryl wondered if they should even be eating and drinking without thought of rationing, but the shock was too much for anyone to think about that right now. She had been studying her colleagues for the last fifteen minutes, watching their hands and mouths, trying to detect guilty gestures that would somehow make sense of all this.

Were they being punished for individual crimes, or was it the company, Alscon, at fault? Monty was a thief by his own admission, but the victim had ultimately been John. Considering her boss's current condition, she didn't imagine he was behind this... *revenge?* What grudge would lead someone to do this to six people? Plus a seventh inadvertent victim.

How had they been so stupid?

How have I been so stupid?

Cheryl had had a bad feeling about the entire thing from the moment she arrived at the farm, yet she'd allowed herself to go along. Peer pressure had led her into a hole in the ground. Now she was stuck.

Mum is going to go mad with worry. What if she never sees me again? Stop being silly, Cheryl. This will all work out fine. It's all a misunderstanding. Sure, my boss just got his hand chopped off, but we're all going to be laughing about it later.

"I was working in a phone shop when John offered me a job," said Monty, breaking the silence. "I sold him a phone and he liked my style. Within my first year at Alscon, I was earning double what I had been flogging iPhones. And what do I go and do? I steal from him. It should be me dying."

"He's not dying," said Alfie, sounding like he was trying to convince himself more than the others. John was in a bad way, and everyone could see it, but as his nephew, Alfie was likely the most devastated of all. "And give yourself a break," he went on. "Alscon is twice the size it was when you joined, Monty, and a lot of that is off the back of sales *you* made. John told me that himself plenty of times."

Monty shrugged. "Maybe."

"He'll forgive you," said Happy, patting him on the knee. "I've known John a long time. He *will* forgive you."

"Maybe not for cutting his hand off though," said Leo. "Think he might stay mad about that."

Happy chided him. "Let's not dwell, shall we?"

Leo nodded in agreement. "Sorry. Hey, Happy, weren't you John's first employee?"

"I was indeed. He and I both worked at a builder's yard as young men. His father died young and left him some inheritance, which is what led him to form his own company. I went with him."

"You're old friends then," said Cheryl, who found it odd because Happy and John didn't act like they were super close in the office. Happy was the guy in charge of the business after John, but as far as she knew, they weren't best men at each other's wedding kind of friends. Happy was pretty much the same with everyone, very friendly and always helpful, but never particularly close. Until this weekend she had know very little about him. After what she had learned about his niece, it made sense. He probably preferred to keep people at a cordial distance than expose them to the pain he must be feeling.

Happy shrugged. "Still just colleagues really, even after all these years. I wanted a better life for myself, which is why I went with John, but the truth is we're very different people."

Cheryl frowned. "How d'you mean?"

"Just different. Anyway, let's hear about you, Cheryl. You've been quite the closed book since joining us. What hobbies do you have?"

She laughed. "Seriously? Well, I can tell you I'm not a fan of team-building weekends. As for what I *do* like, well, um, I can't say anything comes to mind."

"You must enjoy some things, surely? A young girl like you?"

"I used to like horse riding," the admission made her sad for some reason. "I rented a mare at a stable near my house for years — her name was Betty — but after my dad died money got tight and, well, I had to grow up."

Happy nodded as if he understood, and she was grateful he didn't push her to say more. He'd been right about her being a closed book, and she admitted to herself that her failure to fit in at work was her own fault. It was too late to do anything about it now though.

Can't I just rewind three months and start again? Or maybe not even join Alscon in the first place? If I have a Guardian Angel some place, please make that happen.

Anybody?

Alfie was still staring at his uncle glumly. "You know," he said, "Someone could have just taken a piss in the water pistol. Why didn't we think of that?"

Damn, he's right. That would have been nice and simple. Cheryl cleared her throat. "Hindsight won't help us, Alfie. We need to keep moving forward."

"Fine, what do we do next then?"

"We look for the next puzzle," said Leo, "if there *is* one. That, or we wait for that anonymous call to the police in one week. Anyone up for a sleepover?" He winked at Cheryl.

Cheryl rolled her eyes.

Maggie pulled her knees up and hugged them. "How long have we been down here now?"

Leo glanced at the digital clock on the wall. "Just under two hours."

"There goes the prize money," said Cheryl sarcastically, finding it absurd that she'd ever even thought there was any.

Maggie groaned. "It feels like we've been down here an entire day."

"It's the trauma," said Happy. "Seconds last longer in a crisis; but that is what will give us the time to think our way out of this. Do you know that in a crisis, our primal brains take over? We react faster, become less afraid."

Leo chuckled. "And mother's lift cars off of their babies."

Happy didn't laugh. He only grew more serious. "Do you know that has actually happened on several occasions? It's not a myth. When we panic, adrenaline heightens our senses and allows our muscles to contract more forcefully. It literally makes us superhuman. So take solace in that; the more stress we are placed under, the tougher we shall be."

"How do you know all that?" asked Cheryl.

He shrugged. "Crisis management is part of my job. I've done several courses on how to deal with people in stressful situations. In fact, I've done courses on just about everything. I don't have much else to do since my Mandy passed."

"Mandy was your wife?" asked Cheryl. "I'm sorry."

"Don't be. We married at seventeen, childhood sweethearts. I spent twenty-seven years with my Mandy and each day was a blessing. Most people get far less. Thankfully the cancer took her quickly. She didn't suffer. I've been without her six years now."

Cheryl gave a thin-lipped smile. Happy had endured a similar experience to her mother, yet he had found a way to be thankful for what he had instead of broken by what he had lost. Perhaps one day her mother would think like that too. There was hope.

Happy tapped the badge on his lapel. "*Never give up*. Life goes on, but it doesn't last forever. You shouldn't waste a minute of it. Losing my dear Mandy and Polly so close together taught me that. No point in looking back. I'm just glad I got to grow old with my Mandy, and that it was me who taught Polly to ride a bike and tie her shoe laces. I'm grateful that I had those things. Having something is better than having nothing. If I didn't view things that way, I would probably give up."

Cheryl smiled at him. It was a good way to live.

Monty reached forward and took a bottle of water. He tilted it with both hands and sipped. When he finished, he re-fastened the lid and stared at the ground. "I'm not playing this game anymore. I'm going to wait for help, even if it takes a week."

Cheryl sighed. She'd been thinking the same but couldn't see how it was possible. "We lost more than half the supplies," she said. "We'll die of dehydration first."

"Not if we make it last."

"I'm sorry, Monty. There's not enough."

"If we just ration it out—"

"There still won't be enough."

Monty's temper flared like a match being lit. "What the fuck d'you know? You've been acting like Team Leader since this whole thing started. Like you keep saying, you ain't even supposed to be here, so shut your fucking mouth. People are going to find out we're missing. They'll come looking. You negative, fucking bitch."

Leo stopped picking at his blisters and pointed a finger in Monty's face. "Show some goddamn respect, Monty. Cheryl's right, we can't survive a week down here. The way we're going, we won't make it through the day, you prick.

"What d'you call me?"

Leo rolled his eyes. "Oh, don't get your knickers in a twist."

"You want to watch the names you bandy about, bruh. Ain't nowhere to run down here, innit?"

"Come on, Monty," Alfie muttered, getting up to side with Leo. "Chill out."

"This isn't helping," said Happy. "Please stop."

Monty glowered at Leo then looked away. "Whatever."

"We're all going to die down here," said Maggie. "Just look at John. If he dies... If he dies..."

Cheryl watched the woman as she spoke and saw an extremely fragile set of emotions. She was all over the map. "If he dies then what, Mag?"

Maggie peered at Cheryl with wide eyes, still dark beneath the eyelids. "If he dies then this is real, isn't it? If he dies, then we're all going to die too.

"He'll be okay," said Alfie. "John's tough."

She sneered. "No need to tell me."

"What's that supposed to mean?"

"Nothing."

Cheryl put her hand on Maggie to make sure she was okay. "Maggie, what's up?"

She looked at Cheryl with teary eyes. "Nothing is up. I just... If John dies, I-I think it'll be a relief." She gasped and covered her own mouth.

Everyone else seemed shocked as well.

Leo shuffled uncomfortably. "Damn, Mag. That's harsh."

"Yeah," said Alfie. "What the fuck?"

Maggie finally seemed to get her emotions together and settled on anger. It seemed to rise up in her. "He dragged us all into this! I didn't even want to come. I told him that. I told him!"

Cheryl frowned. "So why *did* you come?"

"Because he gave me no choice! If I hadn't come, he would've made my life hell." She rubbed at her forehead. "God, I never should've slept with him. Worst thing I ever did."

"Well, yeah," said Leo. "Sleeping with a married man while you're also married is not a good thing, Mag."

"I agree," said Happy, "but I suspect there is more to it than that, Leo. Maggie, please think before you speak. These might be feelings you don't truly want to share. The situation we're in, the stress... Just be sure you aren't saying things you'll regret later."

Her face contorted into a sneer. "Screw regret. People should know the truth about the man they work for." As quick as it came, her anger spent itself in a flash. Her head dropped as if a heavy tiredness had suddenly overtaken her. "At first, it was a bit of fun. Andrew and I had already been married thirteen years, and every day was the same old routine. No excitement, no surprises, no nothing. It was like I had already experienced everything life was going to offer, and it was depressing. Then I met John — this successful, confident businessman — and he looked at me in ways Andrew hadn't in years. My marriage felt like a prison, keeping me from having any fun or doing anything that I wanted, but John seemed like a way to escape. The night he asked me to work late I said *yes*. I knew what he was planning, and we shagged right there on his desk. I even let him put it in my ass."

Happy grimaced. "Maggie, please, you should stop."

"Yeah," said Alfie. "We know all this. I walked in on the two of you more than once. It's not a secret."

Maggie carried on as if she hadn't heard. It was almost like she was speaking directly to herself, trying to make sense of her own actions. "The affair lasted six months before the guilt got to me. I suddenly realised how much I loved Andrew. My marriage wasn't boring. It was safe and predicable, sure, but those things are not negatives. I realised that excitement wasn't what I wanted after all. In fact, I hated it."

Cheryl gave a thin-lipped smile. "So you broke it off?"

"John left me no choice. He was taking too many risks, almost like he wanted Andrew to find out about us. He would text me at night non-stop and email my personal account instead of work. Once, he even turned up at my house pretending to drop off paperwork. Andrew invited him in and they shared a beer. John seemed to get off on that, and it was then I started hating him. I gave my notice at work, saying I wanted a new challenge somewhere else."

"You quit?" Leo seemed surprised. "Wow, I had no idea."

She shrugged. "I *tried* to quit. John told me if I left he would tell Andrew everything. He had emails and texts from me as proof. So I stayed, but I told him the affair was off. John acted like he understood at first, but he couldn't help himself after a while. He started brushing past me in the office and groping me in the corridors when no one was looking. Eventually we were at it again, only this time around he was rougher. Almost like he was angry at me."

"What the hell, Mag!" Cheryl felt sick to her stomach. "That's rape! The piece of shit has been sexually abusing you."

"What? No, it's not like that. I've never told him no, and I *do* care about him — I think I even loved him for a time. It was my choice to cheat on my husband, and I... I enjoy the sex, but..."

"It's not right, Mag." Leo looked utterly disgusted. "Shit, dude, I quit. No way am I working for John after this."

"Back up," said Monty. "John can't defend himself against any of this bullshit!"

"Yeah," said Alfie. "That's my uncle you're talking about, and he ain't like that."

Cheryl gawped at them both. "Are you kidding me?"

Monty stood up and then pointed a finger. "John's dying here and you're calling him a rapist. What the fuck?"

"Sounds like buyer's remorse to me," said Alfie, glaring at Maggie. "She's probably just working a money angle."

Monty nodded. "Yeah, blackmailing millionaires is good business. Shame on you, Maggie. This is low."

Maggie jolted like she'd been slapped. "Shame on me? Screw you, Monty!"

"Yeah, you'd like that, wouldn't you? Lying cow."

"I'm not lying!"

"Calm down," Happy urged.

"This ain't right," said Alfie, shaking his head. "Just stop talking about it, okay? It ain't right. John's a good bloke."

"It's a pack of lies," said Monty. "Don't let it get to you, Alfie. It's what women do!"

Cheryl groaned. "Way to victim shame, you two. Do either of you have mothers?"

Happy stood up and faced Monty, blocking his view of the others. "Take a time out, Monty. Move away!"

Monty sneered at Happy, towering over the older man and trying to intimidate him, but Happy stood his ground. Finally, Monty tutted and walked to a different corner of the tunnel. Alfie then got up and went with him.

Leo put an arm around Maggie and rocked her. "I'm sorry you've been going through this shit, Mag. We'll make him pay, I promise."

"Yeah," said Cheryl. "We'll make sure the truth comes out."

"Don't do anything," said Mag. "He'll tell Andrew if he finds out what I've said. He'll ruin my life."

"Maybe you should tell Andrew yourself then," said Cheryl. She always thought marriage was about being honest with one another, no matter what. Her parents had always been truthful, and she believed that was why they had never fallen out of love. "But even if not," she said, "now that everyone knows about John, he'd be an idiot to make trouble for you."

Leo sighed. "We'll deal with everything later, but first we need to find a way out of here. No matter what John might have done, right now he needs medical attention."

Cheryl studied her unconscious boss and wondered if the problem would end up resolving itself. She had never seen somebody die before, but she had a feeling John wasn't going to make it through this — not if he didn't get help soon. They had tied off his wrist as tightly as possible, but he remained pale and unconscious.

It was no mystery to Cheryl that men could be predators, viewing women as sexual trinkets instead of human beings, but she'd never been up close to an abuser like this.

But she knew women could be vindictive too.

At school, she'd had a friend named Miranda who claimed to have had sex with lots of different boys, many of whom were in relationships. The chaos she caused resulted in several breakups, but Cheryl eventually discovered one night, when Miranda had been drinking, that she had made it all up. In fact, Miranda was still a virgin.

Men could be monsters, but women could be too.

The revelation caused Cheryl to rewind her judgement for now. While she thought Monty was an asshole — possibly a woman-hating asshole — he also had a point. Their boss wasn't awake to defend himself, and one side of a story did not constitute proof. She focused on something else. Getting the hell out of this hole.

CHAPTER FIVE

ALMOST AN HOUR PASSED by the time they broke from their stupors. John was unconscious, and there was really nothing anyone could do for him, so the duty they felt to stay near gradually fell away. Alfie needed to take a leak, so he snuck off to the end of the tunnel and unzipped his trousers next to the TVR. Leo got to his feet and began walking up and down the tunnel, peering left and right into the various locked cells. Cheryl went to join him in his search. "You okay? You haven't made a bad joke in, like, ages."

"Thought I'd leave you wanting more," he said glumly. "Do you believe what Maggie told us?"

"You've known her and John a lot longer than I have. What d'you think?"

He seemed to give it some thought. "Ask me if John's a sex addict and I'd tell you *yes* in a heartbeat. I've seen the guy cheat on his wife a dozen-times, but that's also his biggest defence. Why would he blackmail a woman to sleep with him when he has no problem pulling girls down the pub half his age?"

Cheryl huffed. "Power. The man Mag described isn't interested in sex, he's interested in power."

"What are you, a psychiatrist or something?"

"No, but I was a psychology student at university for two years. My dad died before I started my third year, but I enjoyed it. I took Feminist Studies as a minor, so I agree I'm a little prone to seeing the worst in men." She chuckled. "I'm not an expert, just thinking out loud. At the end of the day, Maggie and John both cheated on their partners, so both are morally questionable."

"You don't believe in cheating then?"

"Is that a thing anyone *believes* in?"

He conceded the point. "No, I guess not. What I meant was, you never cheated before?"

"No, have you?"

"Never been serious enough with anyone for it to be an issue. It's rare I get to be with one girl, let alone two!"

She shoved him playfully. "You wally. I bet you get plenty of girls."

"You'd think so, but no. I always say the wrong thing. Plus, having Alfie around kind of blinds the ladies."

"Yep, he's a good looking lad, I won't lie, but Leo, you're a handsome guy too. If you stopped with the pervo act, you'd get any woman you wanted."

"Really?"

"Absolutely!"

He grinned. "Wow, look at us, Cher. Are we really doing this thing?"

"What thing?"

"That thing where we give each other backhanded compliments to disguise how badly we want to jump in the sack together. Should we save time and kiss now, or do you want me to play along a while longer?"

She rolled her eyes and groaned. "See? That's why your biggest relationship is with your hand."

"Are you calling me a wanker?"

"I'm stating it categorically."

He looked hurt again, but this time she saw right through it. She grabbed his arm and gave him a little shove. They needed to focus on getting out of there, and flirting would have to come later — if they survived — but she realised she would be open to it. Buried in a hole in the ground, Leo was the only one who made her feel safe, and that had to count for something, right?

"I think I found something over here," he told her, "but I wanted to wait for you to have a look. You're better at this stuff than me."

"Okay, what is it?"

He led her over to another of the cells. This one was unlit, making it hard to see inside. A padlock secured the gate. While he waited for her to take a look, he absentmindedly blew on the back of his hand, reminding Cheryl of his burns. They were obviously bothering him, and it made her suddenly think of something. "Hey, before we get into this, I have something that might help you."

She slid a hand into her pocket and retrieved the Vaseline her mother had given her. Then she handed it over.

Leo seemed perplexed. "What do I do with this?"

"Seriously? Have you never had a burn before? Just rub some on your blisters. It'll soothe the pain. Butter works just as well. I used to get rope burns all the time down at the stables. Mum would always put Vaseline on them."

"Okay, thanks, let me try it." He popped off the lid and slathered a fingertip full of jelly onto the back of his hand. "Hey, that *does* feel better."

"You see?" She took back the Vaseline and slid it into her

jeans again. "So, you want to tell me what you thought was different about this cell? I can't figure it out."

"The numbers on the padlock are blank."

"Really?" Cheryl took the padlock in her hand and studied it. Sure enough, the three rollers on it were blank, cut from white plastic instead of metal. She thumbed at them and found they rolled easily, but without numbers or letters there was no way of knowing the correct combination. She fiddled a moment longer, making sure there were no numbers hidden at the back of the rollers, then ended up shrugging her shoulders. There was nothing — just white plastic rollers with the odd speck of pink discolouration on them that seemed to get worse the more she meddled. It was the discolouration that got her thinking.

"What is it?" Leo asked. "You have an idea, don't you?"

"I'm not sure," she said. "It seems like the paint is wearing off the rollers or..." She thought harder, grasping at an answer rapidly forming in her mind. "It's the moisture from my fingertips. Leo, go get me some water!" It pleased her that he didn't even question her. He rushed off at once and came right back with a bottle of water as demanded. "The only thing we gained from the last cell," she explained to him, "is water and crackers. Pour some water on the padlock."

Leo tilted the bottle and splashed water on the lock. The white plastic rollers turned a solid pink. There were still no numbers on them though.

"Did it work?" Leo looked at her hopefully.

"Hold on." She thumbed at the rollers until...

A white number '**9**' appeared in the middle.

A moment later, she found matching numbers on both the left and right rollers.

9-9-9.

Leo frowned. "Nine-nine-nine? Only thing that means to me is emergency services."

"Me too," she pulled at the padlock and it popped open easily, "but it's the right combination."

When the others heard the squeaking gate, they rushed over. Cheryl couldn't help but smile proudly at yet another success. Maybe she should take a job as a professional puzzle solver.

She looked over at John.

Maybe not.

"Was it unlocked?" asked Monty, peering at the gate.

That deflated Cheryl a little. "No, it was another puzzle. I solved it."

"Well done," said Happy. Nobody else said anything, and it was obvious they were anxious. A new puzzle meant new danger. Whoever had tricked them down here was torturing them on purpose.

Some psychopath with no eyes.

I'm stuck in a crappy horror movie.

"Any volunteers to go in?" asked Leo. "I'll, um, get the next one. Scout's honour."

Alfie huffed. "Pussy."

"You gonna do it then, are ya?" When Alfie squirmed, Leo pointed a finger in his face. "Ha! See? You're ballsack ain't no bigger than mine."

"I'll go," said Monty, stepping forward. "John's hurt because of me. I'll take the risk."

"Technically, you were the one at risk last time," said Leo. "You were the one supposed to lose a hand, remember?"

Monty looked angry, but he bit his lip and took a breath before speaking calmly. "That's why I'll deal with whatever's in there. Let me make things right."

Leo allowed his mocking smirk to drop and he nodded earnestly. "Yeah, okay, man, but you're not on your own. We're all in this together."

Monty nodded. "Move aside, bruh."

Leo stepped aside and Cheryl opened the cell door wider, allowing Monty to go through. For a moment, she felt like an assistant in some bizarre gameshow, and wondered once again if there were cameras on them. The man on the tablet had said he couldn't see them, but who knew for sure?

Who had that man been? Was he badly disfigured or wearing a mask? Were his eyes truly gone? Why was he doing this to them? And did he know she was trapped down there by mistake?

When Monty stepped into the cell, a light came on. There was a small dome sensor overhead, and whatever was inside had obviously been intended to remain a secret until the gate was opened. Now that there was light, the contents revealed themselves.

"I don't like the look of that," said Alfie, clutching himself like a frightened child. His breath misted in front of his face.

Cheryl stared into the cell, trying to work out the puzzle before Monty began. The chair in the centre of the room seemed ordinary enough at first glance, but then she noticed it was bolted to the ground and had clamps around both ankles and armrests. She agreed with Alfie, it didn't look good.

Monty suddenly seemed less eager. "D-Do I just sit down in the chair?"

"Look for an envelope," Cheryl suggested.

"Or a tablet," added Leo. "All the other games have given us at least some clue of what to do. The room seems too big just to have a chair in it."

Monty's quickened breaths became audible. He clearly did not want to go through with whatever came next, but to his credit he did not exit the cell. He searched the room until, eventually, he located a pull cord hanging from the rear wall. He looked back at them nervously through the bars. "S-Should I pull it?"

"Just be careful, dude," Leo warned.

For once, Monty and Leo appeared on the same page and they gave each other a respectful nod. Then Monty reached up and took the cord. "Here goes."

There was a loud *clunk*, and Monty had to duck quickly as something swung at his head. It was a flat-screen television, old and clunky compared to today's models, but still working as evidenced by the screen coming to life. A message flashed up on the display: HAPPY. SIT DOWN TO BEGIN.

Monty frowned. "Does that mean I can't do this one?"

"I guess so," said Cheryl. "D'you think it'll matter if you do?"

Happy stepped into the cell. "It *might* matter, which is why we're better off doing as we're asked. Monty, leave the cell. I'm willing to do this... task. You've had your share of trauma already. Besides, at my age there's not a lot to be afraid of."

Monty seemed reluctant to let Happy take his place, but Happy was unwilling to argue the point. He placed a hand on the much heavier Monty and eased him out of the cell. Once alone, he gave them all a grim smile and sat down in the chair. As soon as he settled, the wrist and ankle restraints snapped into place like metallic teeth. The gate swung shut, locking Happy inside. He flinched but forced himself to keep smiling. "It's okay. I'm okay."

Leo rattled the bars. "He's trapped in there."

The television screen flashed multiple colours like an old-fashioned computer loading a cassette. It was all theatrics because within a few seconds, the eyeless abomination once again appeared. His rasping voice began immediately. "Happy, you have been selected for this task because the associated sin does not include you. Your crime shall be revealed later, so long as your co-workers do not fail you."

Happy's smile dropped for a split-second, and Cheryl

couldn't decide if it was guilt or fear she recognised. It left her uneasy, for as much as you could never truly know anyone, the thought of the friendly old office manager being deviant in some way did not gel with what she knew of him. Happy couldn't be a criminal. It didn't seem possible.

"Retribution has begun," the eyeless man continued, "and while you could accept your fates and do nothing, you have chosen to face further judgement. So be it. One of you is a thief, already revealed. Now it is time to discover another sinner amongst you, a soul shrouded by darker atrocities. One of you is a murderer."

Cheryl instinctively took a step back at the revelation. Could one of her coworkers truly be a murderer?

Monty rubbed at his cheeks, revealing the bloodshot insides of his stretched eyelids. "This one ain't me. I never killed nobody."

Happy was shaking his head indignantly, even as he sat restrained in the chair. "I refuse to believe it. None of us are murderers. We are all good people."

The deformed speaker on the television gave no indication he could hear them. "The cell opposite the one in which Happy now sits is open. Inside you shall find a detailed confession to a remorseless killing, along with directions to the body and other evidence. All the murderer needs to do is step forward and sign that confession. Fail to sign it, and the evidence will be forever buried and the crime shall remain unsolved — but there will be consequences. The killer will have six minutes to confess."

There was a high-pitched *creak*, and Cheryl turned to see the gate to the cell behind them was ajar. She looked up and saw a pair of steel cables running across the ceiling alongside various electrical boxes and flashing LEDs. Whoever was behind these games was some sort of IT whizz, or an engineer. No ordinary person could create a contraption like this.

"I don't think I can go in there," said Monty, realising a new cell had opened. "After what happened with John, and the explosion in the last cell... I'm scared, man. I know I offered to do the task, but..."

It was a display of vulnerability Cheryl didn't expect, and she surprised herself by reaching out and squeezing Monty's hand. His palm was still icy cold. "It's okay. You don't have to do anything."

"I'll check it out," said Maggie. She seemed spaced-out, and her dark eyelids were now nearly black. Her pupils were unnaturally large. "Any objections or shall I just get it over with?"

Nobody objected for nobody wanted to risk getting hurt, but they had to keep playing the game, so if Maggie wanted to volunteer that was fine by them. Otherwise, they were just trapped down a hole with no help coming. Cheryl remembered from her psych studies how important endeavour was to the human condition. They would only be victims if they gave up and accepted their situation. Human beings were happier fighting than dying. Still, it was a surprise that Maggie was the one to step forwards.

Satisfied that no one was going to stop her, Maggie entered the cell. Like the other one, it lit up when she entered. A table sat inside, and on it was a clipboard with a piece of paper. Cheryl had to step up to the bars to see more clearly, but Maggie helpfully explained things from her vantage point. "There's a metal clipboard attached to a cable," she said. "The cable leads into some kind of chute." She picked up the clipboard and waved it at them. It was indeed attached to a steel cable that ran up a chute at the back of the room. Obviously, as soon as the confession was signed, it would be retrieved from above via the chute. Maggie frowned, and then looked at them again. "I can't read anything. It's all covered by a metal plate."

Cheryl squinted to see, and what she saw was a piece of A4 paper sandwiched between a metal clipboard and a silver plate. The silver plate was shorter than the clipboard and, as a result, it left the lower quarter of the confession uncovered. Just enough space for someone to sign their name without being aware of what they were admitting to.

Leo huffed. "If we could read the confession, we might be able to learn what this is all about."

"I suppose only the killer knows," said Cheryl, glancing at the others. "Is there a pen to sign with? I don't see one with the clipboard."

Maggie turned back to search. "Um," she said. "Yes, here!" There was a small pot on the back of the table with a slender, steel pen jutting from it. She snatched it up without examining it first, which proved to be a mistake. Like the clipboard, the pen was attached to a steel cable, and it pulled on something when Maggie yanked it.

A *whooshing* sound emanated from the other cell — the one containing Happy — and Cheryl spun around with anxiety teeming in her guts as she waited to see what came next.

Alfie stared up at the ceiling. "What the hell was that? What just happened?"

"I don't know," said Leo.

Happy blinked and shook his head. Some kind of hatch had opened above him. A cloud of dust descended. Then something dropped from the ceiling and struck the steel floor, making the ground vibrate. Everyone cried out in surprise, but Happy fell to stunned silence. For a moment, Cheryl feared his head might fall off, that something had sliced him in two, but then she saw him struggle and realised he was okay. The object had not fallen *on* him, but *around* him.

Happy struggled at his shackles. "It's some kind of container," he said. "A see-through box."

Cheryl had to squint because it was hard to see, but eventually she was able to make out the perspex container surrounding the chair. Its function wasn't immediately clear.

Until the sand started falling.

It was a slow trickle at first, making Happy splutter and blink, but then it started flowing from the ceiling in a sustained torrent. An avalanche of sand.

Cheryl placed a hand over her mouth. "Oh no."

Happy was trapped inside some kind of nightmarish hourglass. And time was running out.

The sand gathered at Happy's ankles. He tried to break free, but the restraints around his ankles and wrists were unyielding. Panic descended on him. "I'm going to be buried alive. Help me!"

Once again, Cheryl looked at her colleagues, shocked that they held such secrets. Could one of these people she worked with every day for the last three months really be a murderer? Who?

"We need to sign the confession," said Leo, hands on top of his head as he paced back and forth.

"Then sign it," said Maggie. She had become standoffish since her confession about John, and perhaps Happy was right and she was regretting what she'd said.

"I'm not signing it!" said Leo. "I'm not the one who's guilty."

"Guilty of *murder*," said Cheryl, the word staining her mouth. "One of you is a murderer."

"Not me," said Leo. "I haven't killed anyone."

Happy whined from inside the cell. The sand had already

covered his ankles, compacting against the see-through plastic walls. At the speed it was falling, he wouldn't have long.

"I'll sign it," said Monty.

Cheryl gasped. "You killed somebody?"

"No, but what does it matter? We need to save Happy."

"But that's a confession," said Alfie. "You'll be signing your name to a murder."

"You think that shit will stand up in court? I'm signing it to save Happy's life, no other reason. You can all back me up later if we get out of this."

"It would be better if the actual guilty person signed it," said Maggie. "Or maybe you *are* guilty, Monty, and this is just a way of deflecting blame."

Monty sighed. "I don't care what you think, Mag. I never killed anybody, and I'm not about to stand around and let Happy die, you get me?"

Cheryl couldn't take her eyes from Happy. The sand was now piling up against his knees. "Help me," he begged. "Get me out of here, please! Cheryl, I can't die like this. I can't!"

Cheryl realised she had tears in her eyes. She put a hand on Monty's arm and told him to do it. "If we get out of this, I'll back you up the whole way. Just save Happy."

Monty rushed to sign the confession, but he skidded to a halt to avoid colliding with Alfie who stood in his way.

"You can't do this," said Alfie. "It's all a set up. You sign that confession and whatever evidence this psycho has on us will get released. He said there's a body. What if we all die down here, unable to ever defend ourselves."

Cheryl tried to move Alfie out of the way. "What evidence? What body? Do you know something?"

"I don't know shit, but signing a confession is what this psycho wants. We shouldn't be playing along with his sick games. We're being set up, I know it."

Monty turned to look at Cheryl and now seemed unsure. He'd been acting on impulse, but Alfie had caused him to slow down and think. There was no time for that.

Happy cried out. The sand was up to his waist. "I don't want to die. I-I... I don't want to be buried alive. Please!"

Monty shoved Alfie aside. "Happy ain't dying while I can do something about it. Move out the way, bruh."

Alfie was too small to overpower Monty, so he had no choice but to stand aside and let him march into the cell. Monty grabbed the confession and pen, then hesitated. For a moment, it looked like he might change his mind, but then he leaned forward and signed his name with a quick scribble. He turned back to the others. Cheryl nodded to assure him he had done the right thing.

Alfie had his back up against the bars, refusing to look at Happy being buried. "Okay, it's done. Now what?"

Happy wheezed, and Cheryl turned to see the sand covering his belly and rising up to his chest. He was being crushed, and now he begged for help in a winded voice.

She rattled the bars. "We're getting you out of there, Happy. Just stay calm."

He looked her in the eye, utterly terrified, but he chose to trust her and nodded. The sand crept up over the badge on his lapel. NEVER GIVE UP.

Monty was still holding the confession. "Why is nothing happening?"

"Maybe there's a switch or something?" said Leo. He was pacing frantically.

"Then we need to find it." Cheryl rushed into the cell to join Monty, then examined the metal chute secured against the back wall. Ducking down, she peered up inside it and located a tripwire. "Here," she shouted. "Monty, here. Place the confession inside the chute."

Monty slid the clipboard up inside the chute and it flew

out of his hands like it had a life of its own. It disappeared up the pipe, clattering towards the surface.

Happy moaned with relief as the sand stopped falling from the space above his head. He was safe. The game was finished.

Leo sighed and slumped against the bars. "Thank God."

Monty was taking deep breaths, leaning over the table. Cheryl placed a hand on his back and asked if he was okay. "Yeah," he told her, "just wondering what the hell I signed."

"Everything will be okay, Monty. You saved Happy's life, that's what matters."

"Yeah, I know. Is he okay?"

"Let me check."

Happy had been buried up to the hollow of his throat and was struggling to breathe, but no more sand was falling.

Leo rattled the bars, trying to get inside the cell. "Hold on, Hap," he said. "We're going to get you out of there." He glared up at the ceiling. "Hey! Whoever the hell is doing this, we signed your stupid confession, so let our friend go."

The television behind Happy flashed and came back to life. "The murderer has not come forward. An innocent party has signed the confession and a second death will now stain the hands of the murderous coward too meek to take the pen."

More sand began to fall from the hatch in the ceiling. Happy cried out as sand filled his eyes. "No," he shouted, terror-stricken and half-blind. "No, please! Please! I didn't do anything. I didn't do anything!"

Leo shook the bars so hard it looked like he might rip off his own arms. "Happy! Happy, we're going to get you out of there, mate. Happy, stay calm!"

"Help me! Help me, pl—".

The sand filled Happy's mouth and he choked, making the most disturbing sound Cheryl ever heard, like cats being slowly crushed beneath the tyres of a bus. She covered her mouth. "Oh no!"

Happy disappeared in front of them, grain by grain. The sand filled his nostrils and gritted his eyes half-closed — open just enough to see the absolute terror in them.

Leo gave the bars the hardest yank yet, but still the gate refused to open. "Happy, no! We're going to get you out of there. Happy! Happy!"

He was gone, replaced by a container full of sand.

Leo stopped rattling the gates and collapsed backwards into the others. Monty hurried out of the other cell and had to catch him. Alfie slumped against the wall, a look of utter disbelief on his face. "This isn't happening, man. Tell me this isn't happening."

Cheryl burst into tears.

A curtain fell from the top of the cell and obscured their view through the bars, completely removing the horrible scene from sight. It was a small mercy because Cheryl didn't think she could have coped seeing the block of sand with Happy buried inside. Was he still alive in there? Suffocating to death second by second as they wept outside, unable to do a thing about it.

Written on the curtain was a message: **ATONEMENT SLIPS AWAY...**

"How did he know?" Leo asked the question as they sat on the ground, leaning back against the steel container. They had returned to John's side, surprised to see he was still breathing. His wrist no longer bled and he seemed stable, all things considered.

Monty sniffed. There were still tears on his cheeks, and

for the last ten minutes he had been muttering Happy's name over and over. "How did *who* know *what*?"

"How did they know the wrong person signed the confession? Is somebody up there right now?"

"There must be," said Cheryl, staring at the ceiling and imagining the ground above them. Would she ever see it again? "They yanked up the confession and checked the signature. It obviously wasn't the name they were expecting."

"This has been planned for months," said Alfie. "Years even. We aren't getting out of here alive."

Leo winced. "Dude, come on."

"Who's the murderer?" asked Cheryl. "Do we even know who was killed?"

Nobody answered.

"I can't believe Happy is gone," said Maggie. Her hands were trembling in her lap and she no longer seemed angry. Her eyes were bloodshot and she kept wiping her nose.

Cheryl couldn't ignore it any longer. "Maggie, what's wrong with you? You look ill, and your mood is all over the place."

She frowned as though confused. "I'm fine. I'm just coming down with a cold or something."

"Looks worse than a cold," said Alfie. "You look like a crack whore."

"Screw you, Alfie."

Alfie shrugged. He was fidgeting a lot, and it was probably because he was gasping for a fag. That was the least of their problems though.

Cheryl eyeballed Maggie. "You don't look right, Mag. It's chilly down here, but you're quaking like we're at the North Pole. Have you taken something?"

"What? No, of course not. It was just a little something for my nerves. I've been taking them for months now." She saw their concerned expressions and waved a hand dismissively. "They're pills prescribed to me by a doctor. I have panic attacks. I'd show you the packet if I could reach my handbag."

Alfie frowned. "I have panic attacks too. The doctors prescribed me beta blockers. Is that what you've been taking?"

Maggie nodded. "I took one right before we arrived at the farm. I was anxious, being around John, you know?"

"That explains why you changed suddenly," said Cheryl. "When I first got to the farm, you were hyperactive, like an annoying kid, but then you went on a massive downer. They must be strong pills, Mag."

"I already told you, I've taken them dozens of times and never had a problem. It's just a cold." She rubbed at her bloodshot eyes and groaned. "Perhaps I'm going mad. It would explain a lot."

"What do you mean?"

She shrugged as if she'd merely been thinking out loud. "Oh, nothing. It's just that I couldn't find my handbag this morning. I always leave it on a hanger by the door, but it wasn't there when I was ready to leave. Andrew had to help me look for it. He found it in the cupboard under the stairs, but I never put it there — and I could have sworn I had a fresh pill packet in the side pocket, but the pack I found was half empty."

Alfie banged the back of his head against the wall and cursed. "Someone switched your pills, you numpty."

Cheryl glared at him. "Alfie! That's not helping."

"No, he's right," said Leo. "Someone could have messed with Maggie's pills and, like, poisoned her or something."

Maggie shifted onto her knees, ready to get up. It was unclear if she was worried or pissed off. If she planned on bolting, Cheryl was interested to know where. "Why would someone poison me?" she demanded, but then seemed to consider it right there in front of them. Her expression changed from defiance to desperation. "Oh god, what if it *is* true? Maybe I've been poisoned. I-I, yes, I can feel it. I've been poisoned. Oh God."

Cheryl grabbed her to keep her from rushing off in a panic. "Hey, Mag, just stay calm, okay? We have no real reason to think you've been poisoned. We're just talking here."

Mag looked right through Cheryl, bloodshot eyes darting all over the place. "I've been poisoned, I know it."

"No, you haven't. Look, just stay—"

Alfie shrugged and interrupted her. "Happy's dead, why not assume the worst?"

Maggie nodded. "We're all dead. All of us."

Cheryl glared at Alfie. "Shut up, you idiot."

"Maggie? Maggie, I need you!"

They all flinched at the sudden, unexpected sound of John's voice. With no way to help him, they had been focusing on other things — like trying and failing to keep Happy from being buried alive. Now John was awake and looking around in confusion.

Maggie forgot her panic and rushed over to him. "John? John, are you okay?"

"What's happening? Where am I?"

"You're hurt. We're trapped underground."

He wheezed and gave a weak cough. "T-The escape room?"

"Yes, the escape room."

Cheryl was confused by the way Maggie placed a hand against John's cheek. She claimed to hate the man, yet she now seemed to genuinely care for him. Things were likely complicated, she decided.

"I'm sorry," said John weakly. "I... I really didn't know. They said they picked our names at random."

Leo crouched beside Maggie and made John look at him. "Wait, what? You mean it wasn't you who picked our names?"

John shook his head. "When they sent over the invites, they listed six specific names. I asked if they could switch Happy for Jeff from Warehouse, but they said the names were pre-selected from Alscon's website and arrangements had already been made."

"Why didn't you want Happy to come?" asked Cheryl, realising John didn't know his office manager was dead, buried alive by sand.

"I just thought Jeff would have been more fun. Is..." he licked at a pair of extremely dry lips, "is there anything to drink?"

Maggie gave him water from the bottle, which seemed to strengthen him a great deal. It was astonishing how alert he was after being in such a dire way. He seemed almost okay.

Then he realised his hand was missing.

"What? Oh my! How... Is that...?" He tried to rise, but Leo and Monty restrained him. When he looked at Monty, he panicked even more. "Get the fuck off me, you maniac. You tried to kill me. Help! Help!"

Monty stumbled backwards, guilt-stricken and ashamed. Alfie had to take his place holding John down. "Calm down, Uncle John. Monty was just defending himself against *you*. Remember?"

John stopped struggling, and his accusatory glare changed to one of bewilderment. "Jesus, what the hell is going on here? Who's doing this to us?"

Cheryl stood over her wounded boss, wondering how he could be so clueless. "We were hoping you could tell us, John. Happy is dead."

John flinched. "What? No, you're lying. Happy isn't dead. He can't be."

Maggie pulled him sideways into a hug. "He's really gone, John. I'm so sorry."

John let out a wail and the haunting sound filled the entire tunnel. Maggie cradled him in her arms and rocked him back and forth. There were tears in her eyes too.

Leo moved up beside Cheryl and kept his voice low, leaning into her ear. "I thought Maggie hated John. Now she's consoling him?"

"I think she *does* hate him, but I think she loves him too."

"He's really done a number on her, hasn't he?"

Cheryl looked at Maggie, as much a mess as John was, and felt pity. "Maybe he has. Why are *you* here, Leo?"

The question took him by surprise and he frowned at her. She saw the guilt in his eyes then and knew he wasn't innocent, but she needed to know what he'd done. Was he a thief like Monty? Or a murderer?

"W-What do you mean, Cher? I came for the same reason you did — to take part in an escape room. I was tricked down here."

"Come on, Leo. Everyone is here for a reason, that much is clear. What did you do to earn your place? Did you—" She couldn't believe she was about to ask this "—did you kill someone?"

He took her wrist gently, letting his hand slide down until his fingers interlinked with hers. "I'm not a murderer, Cher. Maybe I'm not innocent, like you say, but I'm not a killer."

She felt awkward holding his hand, but she didn't break away. "So tell me what you *are*, Leo. Tell me so I know whether or not I can trust you."

He glanced over at the others, making sure they were out of earshot. Even if they weren't, John's sobs provided cover. He spoke quietly. "You're right, Cher. I am down here for a reason. Blackmail."

"Blackmail?"

"Yeah." He sighed and looked away. "Remember I told you I've seen John cheat on his wife a dozen times down the pub? Well, a few times when he was really wasted, I got out my mobile and filmed him in the act. I made myself quite the video library — even caught him fingering some bird in the toilets once — and when I had enough footage, I kind of, you know, let John know it would be a really good idea if I got a promotion at work."

Cheryl groaned. "You threatened to show his wife the videos if he didn't promote you? Christ, Leo, that is so slimy."

"Hey, you think I don't know that? I just... I got fed up watching John flash his money around and cheat on his wife, you know? I've seen him screw people over left, right, and centre. How do you think he got rich? You think I'm a bad guy, fine, I accept that, but I swear I just wanted to make the world a fairer place. I wanted to bring John down a peg or two."

"To *your* benefit," said Cheryl. She couldn't believe Leo was capable of such behaviour, and it left her disappointed. Maybe she had thought more of him than she'd realised, but it turned out he was just another selfish prick.

But at least he isn't a murderer.

He stared at her now with his deep brown eyes, but they had lost their power over her. "I'm sorry, Cher. I hate to see you think bad of me. I really like you."

She realised he was still holding her hand, but she broke away now. "It's okay. I'm just a little shocked, that's all. I didn't think that you— Hey, wait a minute. You and John are buddies, right? You drink together down the pub together? Am I supposed to believe John would drink with someone who's blackmailing him? Are you lying to me, Leo?"

He looked away, clearly ashamed. "Another of my demands. John buys the drinks for me and my mates. He must have made peace with it because he started to enjoy the abuse." He looked over at Maggie, still fussing over John. "Like her."

Cheryl sighed. The second round of blackmail was somehow worse. Extorting a promotion was a one-time gain, but forcing your victim to drink with you over a sustained period? That was a callous way to behave — to hold power over someone like that.

It's sick.

Leo must have seen the disgust on her face because he grabbed her hand again. "I'll put a stop to it, okay? If we get out of this, I'll make amends. Trust me, I don't much like myself for what I've done, but when it happened, I was a lonely screw-up. I never thought it through. I just saw this selfish man with things I would never have and it got to me. I was angry. At the time, it felt like I was being a hero. Jesus, what the hell was I thinking?"

Cheryl was not a good judge of character, but the self-loathing in Leo's voice sounded real enough. Perhaps he really had made a mistake. Maybe John had needed to be taught a lesson.

She gave him a hug. "If we get out of this alive," she said, "you have a lot of making up to do."

"Yeah, I hear you. My chances of getting you in the sack just plummeted, huh?"

She patted him on the shoulder. "And you were so close!"

There was a strange animal sound and it caused them to turn around. Alfie and Monty were hurriedly clearing a space next to John while Maggie vomited a stream of hot vomit onto the floor. John tried weakly to reach out and help her, but his dismembered hand, still partially attached, twisted and he slammed back against the wall, hissing in pain.

Cheryl hurried to help Maggie, but her convulsions were too powerful to restrain when she got there. Stomach contents pooled everywhere, sending up a foul smell.

"I told you," said Alfie, covering his mouth with his hand. "Somebody switched her pills. She's been poisoned."

Maggie caught a breath between heaves. The whites of her eyes were bloody. "Oh god, please help me. I'm dying."

Leo helped Cheryl hold Maggie while she heaved again, spewing another pint of vomit onto the floor. They looked at one another and shared the same unspoken thought: *This is bad.*

CHAPTER SIX

ALFIE WAS BACKED up against the wall as if he worried the growing puddle of vomit might touch him and make him ill. "What the hell is wrong with her?"

Maggie heaved again. This time only a few strings of saliva hung from her mouth. Her stomach was empty. Now, all she could do was wretch out her own insides. Cheryl tried to soothe the woman, but she was on a different plane — one where only misery and sickness exist. To make matters worse, John's wrist had started bleeding again. His tourniquet had loosened during his attempt to reach out and help Maggie. Monty was busy trying to re-tighten the belt and scarf, but his trembling brown hands turned red with slippery blood.

"We need to get the hell out of here," said Leo, clawing at his bony cheeks in an expression of lunacy. His panic was the most frightening thing of all. His faith that things would all work out okay had finally faltered. "Just let us out," he yelled up at the shaft where the ladder had once been. "Please!"

Of course there was no answer.

Except for a high-pitched beeping.

It sounded like a van reversing, or a particularly petulant

microwave, and yet it took a moment for everyone to notice the sound — Maggie's heaving was still in full force — but once they had, they looked around anxiously.

"What is that?" John asked wearily. He was slumping more and more to his side, near to passing out.

"It's a bomb," said Alfie in a toneless voice, like he was somehow hollow. "We're all screwed."

Cheryl realised no one was going to investigate the beeping — they were all frozen in place — and as it showed no signs of stopping, she climbed to her feet to go take a look for herself. She brushed herself off. "I'll go see what's making that noise."

Monty climbed up beside her, now covered in John's blood. He even had it on his cheeks. "I'll go with you."

She felt better with company, so gave no objection, but was surprised that it hadn't been Leo to offer. He was still struggling to get a grip. Best to let him have some space.

Cheryl moved through the centre of the tunnel with Monty at her left. She took small, cautious steps, her mind conjuring images of spikes shooting up out of the floor and giant boulders dropping on her head. With what had happened to Happy, John, and now Maggie, this was no longer about escaping a room, it was about escaping death.

The beeping came from directly in front of her, and what Alfie had said about a bomb could well be true. An unexpected explosion might suddenly consume her face, or even the whole tunnel, but maybe if she found it she could—

What? Diffuse it? Just cut the red wire, right? Or is it the blue?

She chuckled at the madness of own thoughts and wondered if she was losing her mind. Monty saw her smiling and was understandably confused. "You okay?"

"Sorry, I'm just a bit on edge."

Monty reached out to touch her but hesitated. His hand hovered over her back for a second, and then he tentatively patted her shoulder. "I'm sorry I never made more of an effort to get to know you, Cher. Turns out you're a pretty smart girl."

"Oh, um, thanks. Never too late to make amends, I guess."

Monty laughed, and considering their current situation it was indeed a pretty funny statement. It could well be far too late to make amends.

They got closer and closer to the beeping until she and Monty came to a stop. They looked down by their feet. Was the noise coming from beneath them?

Monty prodded at the steel with the toe of one of his loafers. "You think there's a room underneath us?"

Cheryl bent at the knees and brushed the ground with her fingertips. It didn't feel like there was anything beneath them — the ground felt solid and whole — but the beeping was definitely coming from below. Then she saw it and wondered how she hadn't sooner. "There's a compartment here, look."

Monty eyes widened as he saw what she was pointing to. "Okay, let me take a look. It could be dangerous."

Cheryl found that a little sexist, but she didn't prevent Monty from kneeling. From the way he moved her aside gently, she decided he only wanted to keep her safe.

At the front end of the tunnel, Maggie's retching finally stopped and the beeping became the only sound. John had fallen unconscious again, and Alfie sat next to him, rocking back and forth with an arm wrapped around his knees. Leo was still in a bad way, pressing his forehead against the wall and whispering to himself.

They were all in a bad way.

Monty ran his fingertips around the edge of the compart-ment she had found until he discovered a pair of small grooves in the floor. There was space enough only to insert his fingernails, but it turned out that the panel was only a thin sheet of metal the size of a paperback book. It came up easily.

Inside the compartment, a red bulb blinked in time with the beeping. A small plastic device sat next to the bulb and while Monty probably should have been cautious, he reached right in and grabbed it. A sharp *click* sounded and he froze. "Shite! Shite! Shite! What did I just do? What did I just do?"

Cheryl froze too, not knowing what to expect other than something *bad*, but when a little time passed, she slowly relaxed. She dared to lean forward and stare into the now empty hole. A thick piece of string lay inside, slack and tangled. There was a plastic hook attached to one end.

"It's okay," she said. "It's just a pull cord. It must have been rigged to cut off the beeping because it's stopped now."

Monty examined the small device in his hand. "It's a tape recorder. Should I press *play*?"

"No, let's take it back to the others. We all need to hear whatever's on there."

Monty nodded and turned around. Alfie saw them coming. He pulled his head out of his knees and stared at them hopefully. "The beeping's stopped," he said. "Is everything okay?"

"We found a hidden compartment," said Cheryl.

"With a tape recorder inside," Monty added, holding up the device.

Leo turned away from the wall and seemed to have calmed down a little. "What are the odds it's a message from our congenial, no-eyed host? Can't wait."

Cheryl went to talk to him. There was a fear in Leo's eyes now that hadn't been there before. "Are you alright?" she asked him. She knew it was a stupid question but didn't know what else to say. "Can I do anything?"

His Adam's Apple bobbed as he struggled to speak, and eventually he shook his head. "Everything's just got a little too real, you know? It's getting harder and harder to kid myself that we're all going to get out of this in one piece." He sighed and stared past her. "Look at us, Cher. Mag is dying, John is too, and Happy... What are we going to do?"

"I don't know. I don't know what any of this is about, but we can't lose our sanity, because then it really is over. If there's any chance of us getting out of here, we need to stay focused and together. I need you, Leo. I need you to stay strong for me."

She wasn't even sure if it was true. It'd been a long time since she'd needed anybody, and she no longer trusted Leo wholly, but out of all the people stuck down there with her, she wanted him to be okay. He was the only person she *liked*.

The nod he gave her was slight, and his words were a shallow whisper. "Okay, Cher-bear. I'm back. I'm here."

She smiled and rubbed his elbow. "Nice."

"Shall I play the tape now?" Monty asked from behind her.

"Yes," said John, suddenly rousing from his sleep. "I want to hear it." Maggie had pulled herself across his lap, and her cheek was now on his thigh. Every now and then she let out a pitiful moan.

"Let's do it then." Cheryl took Leo's hand and pulled him into the gathering with the others. They roughly formed a semi-circle and Monty pressed *play*. The tape hissed with interference before a voice emerged. It was not the rasping voice they had expected.

It was not the man with no eyes.

Monty tilted his head towards the speaker and frowned. "Who *is* that?"

Maggie moaned. "Andrew? Andrew, are you there?"

"She's hallucinating," said Alfie. "Be quiet, Mag."

John pointed a finger weakly at the recorder in Monty's

hand. "No, th-that's Andrew. That's Maggie's husband speaking."

Everyone looked at each other. The voice on the recorder sounded ordinary, and even polite; someone nervous about speaking on tape. Was it really Maggie's husband? How was he involved in all of this?

Maggie moaned again. "Andrew? Andrew, I'm so sorry. I love you. Please, come and save me."

Cheryl had a feeling that was the last thing Andrew would do.

Having not paid enough attention after John's shocking revelation about Andrew being the speaker, Monty re-wound the tape and started it again.

Andrew began to speak. "M-Maggie? Are you there? Yes?" He paused and mumbled quietly as if talking to someone beside him. "*This is really weird. I feel uncomfortable.*"

Cheryl took one step closer to Monty, not wanting to miss a single syllable being spoken.

"Maggie, if you're hearing this at some point then you're probably sick. Very sick. Tomorrow, you'll be going on a company weekend with John, but tonight while you sleep I am going to switch your anxiety pills for ones made from refined O-O-Oleander seeds. Y-Yellow Oleander to be precise. Depending on the amount of pills you take, you might die quickly or slowly. There is no reliable antidote, but if you get to a hospital you might have a chance. If you do not find medical help, your heart will seize and you will die."

Maggie let out a moan. Her eyes were open, but it was unclear if she was hearing any of this. John had his hand on her arm and was clutching her tightly.

"Maggie, I've always loved you — I love you even now —

but I can't put up with your lies any longer. Do you really think I don't know about you and John? I know, Maggie. I've known for a long time. That piece of shit even came to our house. He drank a beer with me while you watched. Did I really deserve that? Did the two of you laugh at me afterwards? Andrew, such a naive fool."

Monty shook his head at John. "Somebody always gets hurt, bruh, innit? You muppet."

"I waited for you to end it," Andrew continued, "but you never did — so *I* will end it. You can both die in that room. Justice demands it."

The tape ended.

Alfie placed a hand against his forehead and his gelled black hair fell forward in front of his face. "This is all her fault. We're down here because Maggie's a fucking whore!"

"Hey!" Cheryl glared at him. "Your goddamn uncle is just as much to blame."

"*More* to blame," said Leo. "John has been fucking around with women for years. It finally caught up with him."

Alfie folded his arms and looked away.

"I'm s-sorry." John mumbled a few more words, then his eyes rolled up in his head. He was out again.

Alfie was on his feet, pacing angrily. "So why the hell have we been dragged into this? What the fuck did we do? I never even met Maggie's husband."

"Maybe it's because you all covered for them?" Cheryl suggested, trying to make sense of it herself. "Maybe Andrew thinks *everyone* here is to blame."

Alfie shocked her then by giving her a nasty shove. "Shut the fuck up. What the hell do you know?"

Monty grabbed Alfie. "Calm down, bruh."

"Sod off, you fucking thief." Alfie swung a fist at Monty, but Monty ducked and delivered his own. It struck Alfie in the ribs and dropped the lad like a sack of spuds.

Leo leapt in front of Monty and broke things up before any more blows were exchanged. "He's just freaking out. Give him a minute."

Alfie sobbed on the ground and clutched his ribs. "I want to go home. I don't want to die down here."

Monty stared at his bloodstained hands and suddenly seemed ashamed of lashing out. He crouched next to Alfie and put a hand on his back. "I'm sorry, Alfie."

Alfie shrugged him off. "Leave me the fuck alone."

Monty sighed, but did as he was told. He went and spoke with Cheryl. "So it was Andrew who tricked us all down here? Didn't see that coming."

Cheryl was almost convinced now that she would never see daylight, yet she wasn't entirely satisfied with the reasons why. It didn't make sense that Andrew would take revenge on all of them — surely revenge against John and Maggie would be enough. Also, how could he have built something like this in secret? Was his marriage really so bad that he could sneak off to bury a bunch of shipping containers and rig them with games?

Not games. Traps.

Cheryl went over to John. His skin had turned the colour of yellow chalk left to fade in the sun. "John," she said, trying to rouse him. "John, wake up. What does Andrew do for a living?"

John blinked lazily, and his eyes took a while to focus on her. "Cher? What is it?"

"Maggie's husband; do you know what he does for a job?"

"He works at a... at a post office."

Leo gave her a nudge to get her attention. "What does it matter?"

"I'm not sure it does," she admitted. "I just don't think Maggie's husband did all of this. When would he even have got the time? This has to be about more than Maggie's marriage."

"It sounded like he was with someone when he made the recording," said Monty, seeming to agree with her. "Maybe he was forced to do it. He sounded nervous."

Cheryl thought so too. Andrew hadn't sounded like a man who enjoyed making grand speeches of vengeance. His tone had been jittery. His words had sounded rehearsed. "Maybe he's a victim in all this as well."

Alfie stopped clutching his ribs and held a hand out so that Leo could help him to his feet. Once standing, he brushed himself off and looked at them. "Andrew wanted Maggie dead. He switched her pills, didn't he? If he knew about her sleeping with John, he would want revenge on everyone who knew about it. You heard him mention being laughed at. He wanted to settle the score."

"Not like this," said Cheryl. "This is madness."

Alfie shrugged. "What does it even matter? We're all dead."

"Then what's the point of all this?" Monty asked. "Why all of the games?"

"To make us suffer all the more."

Cheryl still wasn't happy with the theory. It didn't fit. This was about more than Maggie's marital problems. It had to be. "We're missing something. Andrew said Maggie might have a chance if she gets to a hospital. Why go to the trouble of explaining that? Why not just say there was no cure and that she was going to die down here? Why mention the possibility of getting help if there isn't any?"

"Because there's still a way out?" said Leo, understanding what she was thinking. "Seems like a bit of a stretch, but maybe."

"There are more cells," said Cheryl, "and this doesn't feel like the end to me. We're missing something."

Leo stared down the tunnel. "Should we try and open another cell? Find another game?"

She nodded. "Monty, is there anything written on that recorder? A number or something? A new clue?"

Monty rotated the small device and studied it from all angles. "There's nothing on it. Hey, wait a sec though, let me check something." He pressed one of the buttons and the deck opened up with a *clack*. Inside was a tiny cassette, not like the clunky ones her dad had used to store in boxes in the loft and insist would be valuable one day. Monty gave it a quick examination and then slid it back inside the recorder. He grinned at them as he pressed the *play* button. "B-side, innit?"

For a few seconds there was nothing but a crackling silence. Then a voice they all recognised started to talk. It was the man without eyes. "God judges the adulterer, and all of you have indulged in the sin of infidelity, deepening the wounds of its innocent victim. Margaret, Johnathan, today is your reckoning, along with all those who have abetted you."

Alfie threw his head back and swore. "Why are we to blame for them two fucking around? This is bullshit, man."

The recording continued despite his protests. "Murder, theft, adultery; transgression already unveiled. Yet another sin festers, a boil waiting to be lanced. Confess and live. Atone or die. Ask for forgiveness and make good your sins."

They waited several minutes, but no more words were spoken. The recording ended.

"Make good your sins," said Leo. "You think that's the next clue?"

"It's the only thing that sounded like one," said Cheryl. "Check the cells."

They got to work, knowing the drill by now. It took less than a minute for Monty to find something. "This padlock has a code on the back."

They walked over to join him, and Leo examined the padlock for himself. On the back was a series of numbers and letters — all 26 members of the alphabet listed in order, starting with 1 for A and 26 for Z. "What makes you think this is the right cell?" Leo asked.

Monty pointed inside. On the back wall was a glowing red sign made from LEDS and transparent tubing. It read: ATONEMENT.

Leo nodded. "Yeah, fair enough. So what's the riddle? What's the game?"

"We have to spell something out using the code," said Monty. "Agreed?"

Cheryl thought he was onto the right track, but she was determined to contribute something herself. There were already numbers dialled into the padlocks — **19, 9, 14, 19** — and she wondered what they translated too. She didn't expect they were random. "Hey, Leo, can you use your numbers-brain to check what word this combination spells?"

Leo took the padlock from Monty and held it in his hand, turning it back and forth so he could see both the combination and the code. Slowly he deciphered the word on the padlock. "S-I-N-S."

"Okay," said Cheryl. "Give me a sec. Sins, sins, sins... *Make good your sins.* That's it! Change the combination so that it spells 'good.'

Leo thumbed the rollers, working out the right numbers by using the code on the back — **6, 15, 15, 4.** The padlock popped right open.

Cheryl pushed the gate, opening up the cell. "Looks like we're still in the game."

———

Like the other cells, this one lit up as soon as they entered.

The small space was packed with video cameras, all pointed at a bizarre structure in the centre of the room.

Monty moved protectively to the front of the group. "What is that? It looks like a coffin."

It did resemble a coffin, wide at the top and tapering towards the bottom, but it was made out of metal — dimpled brass, by the looks of it. It was also too short to be a coffin. There was a wide hole at the top at about shoulder height. The structure's purpose was unclear, but then she saw an envelope stapled to its side. She hurried inside the cell and opened the envelope. She read aloud the letter inside. "*Alfie, your sins are buried. Unearth them and be set free.*"

Alfie backed away from them and started hyperventilating. "I-I ain't doing it, man. Whatever it is, I ain't doing it."

Monty stalked him. "You have to, bruh. What choice do we have?"

"I ain't doing it! No way, I'm not ending up like Happy."

Leo went after him too. "I know you're scared, dude, but we'll be right here. You can do this."

"We're never getting out of here, you idiots!" Alfie suddenly seemed so young, just a boy. "We're going to die down here, don't you see?"

"Then what do you have to lose, bruh? Get it over with, yeah?"

"No!"

Leo tried to put an arm around Alfie but missed and stumbled. "Come on, dude. We all have to take our turn."

"So *you* go in there then, Leo. Let's see how brave *you* are."

"The letter had your name on it. It has to be you, Alfie."

Alfie stopped backing up and raised his good hand as if to fight them. "Cheryl could have been making it up for all I know. It might not even be my name."

Cheryl marched over to Alfie and shoved the letter against his chest. She waited for him to read it.

He shrugged. "Yeah, well, so what? I still ain't going in there."

"You either go in voluntarily," said Monty, "or I'll drag your pussy-arse in there myself."

Cheryl voiced her disapproval. "Monty, there's no need for that."

He glanced back at her. "If he doesn't get in that cell, we'll all starve down here. You're the one saying we need to play the game if we have any chance of getting out."

Leo looked at her apologetically. "I'm with Monty. Alfie needs to get in that cell one way or another."

"Touch me and I'll knock you the fuck out." Alfie raised his fist higher. "Just try me."

This is getting bad, thought Cheryl. In closed confines like this, a fight breaking out could be deadly. There was no one to break it up and no one to get help. She had to stop things from escalating. Stepping into the middle of the posturing men, she attempted to reason with Alfie. "If you do this, Alfie, you can relax. This is your turn, but once it's over it will be somebody else's. You already know things are bad, but this is your chance to do the right thing and help us. It's not going to go away, so just face it and get it over with."

Monty allowed his posture to soften. "Look, bruh, don't be a pussy like me. John is dying because I didn't take my turn. If you don't take yours, something bad is guaranteed to happen, but if you play the game and manage to win then maybe we have a chance of getting out of here."

A tear spilled down Alfie's cheek. "I'm scared, man. Please don't make me go in there."

Monty pulled him into an embrace and patted him on the back. "You can do this, Alfie. You're my mate, and I know you can do it."

To Cheryl's surprise, Alfie started nodding. She'd been

sure things would devolve into violence, but they now seemed to be heading away from that direction.

Alfie sobbed quietly as he moved over to the cell. He hesitated before going inside, but not for long, and it seemed he had made up his mind to go through with whatever came next.

"So what do I do?" he asked, looking back at them. "Do I mess with this metal thing?"

No one answered because no one knew the answer. Also, they were afraid — perhaps not as much as Alfie, but enough to take the words from their mouths.

Deciding to just go ahead and try something, Alfie moved around to the back of the brass coffin and started fiddling with it. He soon managed to open a rear compartment, and it became clear what he was supposed to do.

"I'm supposed to climb inside."

"We're here," said Cheryl. "We're right with you, Alfie."

He gave them an anxious glance, then climbed into the coffin's interior. His neck slotted into the hole at the top, leaving his head exposed and his body enclosed. The back casing snapped shut, trapping Alfie inside. Tears and snot covered his face. He looked like a sad Russian doll.

"It's okay," said Cheryl. "We're right here."

As if to mock her words, the cell door swung shut, locking them out. Alfie was on his own.

"What now?" Alfie tried to keep his voice from descending into sobs. "Nothing's happening."

The light in the cell went out and so did the red tubular sign. Alfie screamed in the darkness. They could no longer see him.

"Something is happening, all right," said Monty. "Just stay calm, Alfie. We'll get you through this. It's just a game."

A spotlight sliced through the darkness, casting a yellow

cone over a terrified Alfie. Then the cone shifted, moving away from Alfie and settling on the back wall.

It wasn't a spotlight. It was a projection.

The man without eyes stared back at them and began to talk. "Alfie Maguire, you are guilty of a grievous crime, and through its undertaking a family has been denied closure. Yet your crime was in service to another, a transgression intended to obscure one even more heinous. Confess your sin, Alfie, and seek atonement. Only then shall you be free."

The projection shifted back down, once again illuminating Alfie and the brass coffin.

Alfie struggled, his neck bulging against the metal edges of his cramped prison. "What sin? I haven't done anything. Let me out of here."

Cheryl grabbed the bars and poked her face through the gaps. "Alfie, don't mess around. We know this is real, so just confess whatever crime you can think of."

"There's nothing," he protested. "What do you want from me? I wank off in the bath. I don't always wash my hands after a piss. I don't deserve to die."

"You must know something, Alfie. The psycho who trapped us down here wants to hear something in particular. What sin does he know about? Why would he want revenge on you?"

"I don't know who the fuck *he* is?"

Leo shushed them. "Quiet! I hear something."

A hissing sound filled the silence.

"Oh God," said Alfie. "What is that? Snakes?"

"No," said Cheryl. "It's gas."

Suddenly a spark ignited and a flame *whooshed* to life. It rose underneath the coffin, licking at the bottom.

Alfie's face quivered in terror. "What's happening?"

"There's a fire," said Leo. "Underneath you."

"Oh fuck oh fuck oh fuck."

Cheryl told him to stay calm. It didn't work.

Hanging from the ceiling, half-a-dozen video cameras lit up and began whirring, filming Alfie's predicament.

"You need to give a confession," she shouted through the bars. "That's what he wants."

"I have nothing to confess!"

"Alfie, you must have something."

"I don't!"

Cheryl turned aside to look at Monty and Leo. "Do you know what he did? Do you know what he needs to confess to? Now is the time to stop covering for him."

Leo shook his head. So did Monty, but she was less inclined to believe him. He and Alfie were both in sales, thick as thieves. Mates. Buddies. *Brethren.*

"Monty," she said, staring him in the eye and trying her best to sound stern. "You saw what happened to Happy. We have to follow the rules. Help Alfie. What does he need to confess?"

"I swear I don't know."

"Damn it, Monty, I don't believe you. He's your friend."

His face twisted in anger, but he fought it off and gave her a pleading look. "I promise you, Cher. I don't know what he did."

"Get me out of here!" Alfie was yelling now. "I can feel it getting hot. I'm going to burn to death in here. Come on!"

The brass coffin started to glow at the bottom. It was heating up like an old-fashioned kettle. And Alfie was stuck inside it. He began to sweat, beads on his forehead catching the light like jewels. His slick black hair whipped back and forth in front of him as he thrashed.

"Confess!" Cheryl shouted. "Don't die in there, Alfie."

The cameras overhead continued to whir, and Alfie seemed to notice them for the first time. Instead of confessing, he swore and cursed at their lenses, calling out the man who had put him there. Was he watching this? Or would the footage be retrieved later?

Monty rattled the bars. "Alfie! I need my sales sidekick, innit? Do what you have to do to get out of there."

Alfie whipped his focus to Monty and glared. "I ain't your fucking sidekick, Monty. Half the sales you get are stolen. You use John's login details to steal everyone else's leads. You think I'm stupid?"

Monty's mouth fell open. "W-What...?" He took a moment to breathe. "Yeah, okay, you're right, Alfie, you got me, hands up, I've been doing it for years. Monty Rizwan is a piece of shit who looks out for number one. A thief too. Oh, and I hacked off my boss's hand. All in all, I'd say my future is pretty much over, yeah? This ain't about me though, bruh. This is about whatever shit *you're* guilty of.

"I ain't guilty of— Shit! It's getting hot. Help me, man, please!"

"Help yourself, bruh!"

Leo tried pulling at the gate, just like he had when Happy had been getting buried alive. It didn't do any good this time either. The brass coffin started to glow red. Alfie's eyebrows dripped sweat.

Cheryl yelled again. "Alfie, time is running out. You have to confess to something."

He didn't seem to hear her. He thrashed wildly, like he hoped to squeeze his body out through the head hole. "It's burning me. It hurts. Get me out of here. Get me out of here. Get me out of here."

"Just confess," begged Cheryl. "What's the worst thing you ever did?"

Alfie went bright red in the face. The glowing heat at the bottom of the coffin climbed upwards, inch by inch. He was going to burn alive.

Alfie screamed.

Then he confessed.

"I buried a dead girl," he shouted at the cameras. "I-I buried a body so that nobody would ever find it. I helped cover up an accident." He screamed in pain. "N-N-No, a murder. I helped cover up a *murder*."

The flames continued burning. The heat continued rising. Alfie's eyes rolled about in his head. Why wasn't it over? Why wasn't he free? He had just confessed to covering up a murder.

"Who was it?" Cheryl yelled through the bars. "Who was the dead girl?"

"Wh-what?"

"Who's body did you bury?"

"Polly," said Alfie, screaming between the words. "P-Polly McIntyre."

The flame disappeared. The back panel of the brass coffin sprung open. Alfie collapsed, dropping backwards out of sight. Cheryl rattled the bars of the gate and stumbled in surprise when it swung open.

Monty and Leo raced into the cell and retrieved Alfie. They grabbed him by the arms and dragged him into the centre of the tunnel. His trainers, and the ankles of his skinny jeans, were smoking and the smell of bacon wafted though the air. Cheryl patted Alfie down. He moaned in pain.

The skin on his shins had melted into the denim of his jeans. His feet were bubbling in his shoes.

"I don't think you have enough Vaseline for this," said Leo, looking at Cheryl with a queasy look on his face.

"No," she said. "I don't."

CHAPTER SEVEN

CHERYL WAS DYING to question Alfie about his confession, to ask about Polly McIntyre — was it the same Polly who disappeared? Happy's niece? — but she couldn't. Alfie was hurt badly. The pain was too much for him to focus. Tears leaked all over his face as he writhed on his back, and every time someone spoke to him he replied only with moans.

"I feel like we're dropping one by one," said Leo, and he nodded at where John and Maggie were still lying, close to death. They were positioned side by side, holding hands as if they knew their time was coming. They didn't speak, they didn't move, they only stared into space, blinking every now and then. Cheryl expected both of them to die and it horrified her. She had never *expected* anyone to die before. Death had always been a nasty surprise. Something that happened out of nowhere. Something that happened without warning.

Her dad had just been making bacon sandwiches. An ordinary afternoon. His final afternoon.

I'm sorry, sweetheart. The doctors said it was instant. There was nothing anyone could have done.

He's gone.

Death had always been a surprise for Cheryl.

Until today. Today she saw it coming, approaching down a narrow alleyway with no hope of escaping it.

Monty shuffled onto the ground between her and Leo and passed around some crackers. There was a bottle of water too that they had used to douse Alfie's legs, and she reached for it now, sipping a few mouthfuls greedily. Then she crunched on a cracker, the best cracker she had ever tasted.

"You okay?" Monty asked.

She nodded, but told him, "Not really."

"I hear that."

Leo chuckled through a mouthful of cracker, his angular chin pistoning back and forth. "It's down to us three. Think we'll win a prize?"

"Just show me daylight," said Cheryl. "That's good enough for me."

Monty looked at his watch. "You'll have a wait on your hands. It's passed seven."

Cheryl gasped. "Is it really that late? No wonder I'm so exhausted."

"Wanna take a nap?" Leo winked and patted his lap.

"Seriously? You just watched one of your coworkers almost get burned to death."

"*Almost* to death."

Monty chuckled. "I suppose, if nothing else, it shows we can survive this by following the rules. Maybe we really can get out of here if we play along with this psycho's games."

Cheryl had considered the same thing. If the games were fair then perhaps they really would be released if they managed to survive them. After all she'd seen, it seemed unlikely. It would be crazy to let someone go after torturing them. Even if Maggie's husband was just a pawn in whatever was going on, he at the very least would go to jail. Happy was dead, even if the rest of them got away.

And that's a big even.

"Alfie's alive because he admitted to murder," she said. "Was Polly McIntyre Happy's niece?"

Leo nodded. "Yeah. I can't believe Alfie killed her. I always thought it was you, Monty."

"What? Shut your mouth, bruh. I ought to mash you up."

Cheryl looked at Monty. "Why would Leo suspect you?"

"Because I had a barny with Polly the night she disappeared."

"What about?"

He shrugged. "No clue. I don't remember anything about that night, but I know I didn't hurt Polly. I wouldn't. The police had me in their sights for a while because my car had been wrecked the same time she had vanished, but even they eventually decided I had nothing to do with it."

Leo nodded. "Yeah, well, the mystery has been cleared up now. Alfie killed her."

"No," said Monty. "He said he was involved, but didn't admit to killing her, only that he buried her body."

Leo shrugged. "So what? He must've killed her in order to bury her."

Monty shook his head. "Nah, bruh. That's not what he said. I reckon someone else killed her and Alfie helped cover it up."

Cheryl asked a question that needed asking. "*Who* then? Who killed Polly?"

"John probably," said Leo, "or maybe it was Happy."

"What? But Polly was his niece."

"Exactly. Aren't most murders committed by someone the victim knows? Family or friends?"

Cheryl frowned. "Happy's dead. Why continue with this torture if the murderer has been punished?"

No one answered for a second, but then Monty provided a theory. "The game has kept on going because everyone is guilty of something. I'm guilty of thieving from Alscon," he glanced at Alfie lying on the ground nearby, "and my coworkers. Alfie is guilty of hiding Polly's body. I suppose John and Maggie are guilty of adultery. That leaves Happy and Leo."

"And Cheryl," said Leo.

"No, bruh. She ain't meant to be part of this, innit? So it's either you or Happy what murdered Polly, I reckon."

Leo shuffled around on his butt so that he was facing Monty. "What? I didn't kill Polly, you moron."

"Well, you must have done something."

"He blackmailed John," said Cheryl. "He admitted it to me earlier. He's been exploiting John with threats of exposing his cheating to his wife."

Monty studied Cheryl and then studied Leo. Then he shrugged. "There you go then, Happy must have killed his niece."

"So there's nothing left to hide," said Cheryl. "We need to find the next game and just admit everything. It's our only chance."

Leo leaned his head back against the wall and sighed. "Finally, this might be over."

"Hold up," said Monty, "something still doesn't add up. There was a confession the murderer was supposed to sign."

"Yeah," said Leo, huffing. "*You* signed it."

"Yeah, bruh, but I only signed it to save Happy, innit? Happy was stuck in that chair being buried alive by sand."

"Because it wasn't his sin," said Cheryl, understanding what he was getting at. "Happy was made to sit in the chair because he *wasn't* guilty of the murder. The confession wasn't for him."

"So I guess we don't know everything after all," said Leo, looking downcast.

"Let's not assume we've got this all figured out," said Monty.

Cheryl sighed. "You're right. We shouldn't get ahead of ourselves. There's clearly more to this than we understand."

"But we do know one thing," said Monty. "Polly didn't disappear, she was murdered — and Alfie knows who the killer is. Anybody up for getting some answers?"

Cheryl looked at Alfie, moaning on his back and sobbing with pain. It would be cruel to badger him, but when she thought about him burying the body of an innocent young girl, she suddenly didn't care. "It's time for people to stop keeping secrets," she said. "I want to hear the truth."

Cheryl knelt by Alfie's head, wanting to look him in the eye as he answered their questions. His confession must have been true because his torture had ended as soon as he'd spoken Polly's name. It must mean someone could hear them, and they knew when Alfie had admitted what they'd wanted to hear. They weren't alone down here in the tunnel.

And yet Cheryl had never felt so isolated, so vulnerable. She wanted her mother so badly it hurt and being smothered would never again be a burden if she got out of this alive.

Hell, I'll happily never leave the house again.

Just need to stay strong, Cher. Need to find my way out of this situation.

Monty gave Alfie a tap on the arm to get his attention. Despite his pain, Alfie was lucid, and looked at Monty right away. "You gotta get help for me, man. I need a hospital."

"There's no help coming," said Monty callously. "So just deal with it. We need you to do some explaining."

"Please man, just—"

"Shut up, bruh. Tell us what you know about Polly. Did you kill her?"

"What? No, I swear. Just help me. *Please*, man."

"We *can't* help you," said Cheryl. She looked down at the sticky patches of bright red skin peeking through his ragged jeans and winced. "We're trapped, you know that. Our only way out is to tell the truth, so tell us what you know."

"I don't know anything."

Monty gripped Alfie's ankle and squeezed. "Listen up. Polly was a cool chick and I liked her, so start speaking or I'll mash you up."

Alfie gritted his teeth to keep from bellowing. He closed his eyes and shuddered but managed to nod. "Okay, okay, I'll tell you. I didn't kill her, okay? I swear."

"But you buried her," said Leo with a snarl.

"I buried her, yeah."

Cheryl didn't understand. "Why?"

"Because he made me! He made me bury her so no one would know what happened."

Cheryl grabbed Alfie's arm, growing frustrated. She shook him. "Who asked you to bury Polly's body?"

Alfie clenched his jaw as if he intended not to answer, but when Monty grabbed his ankle again he had no choice. "Uncle John! It was John who asked me, all right? He killed her. I just... He threatened to blame it on me if I didn't help him and said I would have a job for life if I helped make it go away. He gave me twenty-percent of Alscon. You know how much the company is worth? Three-mil."

Leo whistled. "Half-a-million quid in stocks to bury a body. I'd have been tempted myself."

Cheryl glared at Leo, intended to chide him, but when she thought about that kind of money, she couldn't judge with an entirely clean conscious. Polly had already been dead, after all.

What the hell am I saying?

"Why did John kill her?" she demanded.

"It was an accident. She stumbled out of the bushes right

into the middle of the road and John ran her down. It was the night of the staff do, the night at the Claybrook Estate. We were all wasted, man. She must have been drunk too. It was just an accident. Please—"

Cheryl shook his arm again. "Why not call the police? Huh?"

"Because John had been doing champagne and coke all night. He should never have been behind the wheel. Plus Maggie had been in the passenger seat sucking him off."

Cheryl recoiled. "Jesus! You sick people. You goddamn si—"

"Hold up," said Leo, raising a hand. "What d'you mean John ran her down? A limo took us all to the Claybrook that night. No one drove there."

Alfie managed to get up on one elbow, and he shook his head. "Monty drove his TVR. He didn't want his family knowing he was going to drink."

Leo huffed. "Yeah, and if I remember right, Monty ended up more wasted than anyone. It was the same night he wrapped his car around a tree."

Monty looked away, ashamed, but he didn't deny it.

Alfie was shaking his head again. "Monty never drove that night. It wasn't him that wrote off his car. It was John." He looked at Monty now. "You were passed out in the hotel's lobby by half-ten. John called you a lightweight and took your keys for a laugh. Maggie wanted to see how fast the TVR went, so John took her for a spin. I was having a fag on the front steps when they left and I watched them burn it away down the driveway. It was a really long access road, remember? Went right through a load of woods and past a pond."

Monty didn't reply. His mouth was open and his eyes were wide and unblinking.

"I remember it," said Leo. "How did John and Maggie

manage to hit Polly all the way out there? Was she partying with them?"

"Honestly, I don't know," said Alfie. "I got a text just after midnight telling me to meet him at the pond. I didn't find out what had happened until I got there. John said she stumbled out of the bushes and into the road. He'd been doing over sixty when he hit her, and then he had skidded into a tree. Somehow, he and Maggie were okay, but they were both covered in bruises. Polly was lying in the trees, but there wasn't anything they could do. By the time I got there Maggie was in hysterics, but John was frightening. I thought if I refused to help him, he might kill me too. Drown me in the pond or something."

"So what did you do with her body?" Cheryl felt sick to her stomach. Alfie wasn't even twenty and he'd helped dispose of a corpse. Was he a victim too? Or as evil as John?

And what about Maggie?

"There was a bonfire nearby," Alfie told them. "I tried to burn her body there amongst the wood with my lighter, but it was taking too long and the fire kept burning out. I was out there so long the sun started to rise. I panicked and dragged her body over to this old shipping container full of broken lawnmowers and stuff. I found a shovel and dug underneath it, buried her there. For months I was sure her body would turn up, but no one found her. After a year, I snuck back onto the estate and went to check on the container. It was still there, full of the same old gardening equipment."

Monty's lower lip was curled in disgust. "The police questioned us for months, bruh. John put up a ten-grand reward for information. You've kept up a lie for nearly two years. How do you sleep at night?"

"By drinking and partying. You think I'm okay with it? I liked Polly too, man. I asked the girl out the week she started."

"Yeah," said Leo, "and she turned you down. Must've felt like you had the last laugh."

"Get stuffed, man. You asked her out too. In fact I remember you had a right thing for her. We all tried to get with her."

Cheryl groaned. "Jesus Christ, I can't actually be hearing this. Yesterday you were all just a bunch of people I worked with, and now..." She stood up instead of finishing her thought. Leo reached for her hand but she dodged away. She didn't want to be touched. She needed space.

She needed air.

She needed her mum.

And more than ever, she needed her dad. What would her life have looked like if he hadn't left her?

None of this is supposed to involve me. I never even met Polly.

Without thinking, Cheryl found herself inside the cell with the brass coffin. Her eyes caught the video cameras above and she yelled at them. "If this is all about an innocent girl, then you're a hypocrite. What the hell am I doing down here? What did I do? Let me out of here because I'm innocent too, just like Polly was."

The cameras' lights were no longer on. Their mechanisms no longer whirred with life. No one was listening, no one was watching. She wandered back out of the cell and into the tunnel. They had done as requested — Alfie had confessed — so what came next?

More games?

What would be the point? The truth was out now. Alfie's confession had been recorded. Her co-workers were a bunch of criminals, ranging from petty theft and blackmail to murder and unlawful disposing of a corpse. Their secrets were out.

I need to get out of this hole and as far away from these people as possible.

Just need to convince a psychopath to release me from his dungeon first.

She sensed Leo move a few feet behind her. He probably wanted to check on her, but his crimes sickened her. And yet she still found herself liking him. Leo hadn't buried a body like Alfie had, or run down a girl like John. He had behaved like a bit of a snake, but if he owned his mistakes didn't he deserve forgiveness? And what about Monty? He was no murderer either, just a chancer and a thief. Whatever her co-workers had done, they were human, and she reminded herself that they were all stuck in this situation together. They had to stay on the same side for now. She had to ignore their crimes as best she could.

Someone was trying to kill them all. The point of these games was to extract confessions, but part of her knew that the trick at the end would be them never getting out. The more she thought about it, the more she imagined them all disappearing off the face of the earth, their confessions published all over the internet with no way to refute them. This torture chamber wasn't for their benefit, not a chance to atone, it was for whoever had led them down here. It was for the amusement of a twisted psychopath.

Cheryl turned and made an announcement. "No more games."

Alfie glanced up at her from the floor. He had managed to sit up and was looking at his own charred legs in horror. "What are you talking about?"

"I mean you've been right all along, Alfie. We're all going to die down here. Every time we play along with this psycho's rules, someone gets hurt or killed. This whole thing is revenge, and the more we play by the rules the worse things get. So no more playing by the rules. We're finding a way out of this mess."

Leo nodded, his square chin jutting out defiantly. "I agree. This game is rigged."

Monty bashed his fist into his palm, and for the first time ever since meeting him, he gave her a warm, genuine smile instead of a smarmy smirk. His defences were down, and the real Monty Rizwan was on display. She liked him.

Alfie reached up to Leo and took his hand. He pulled himself onto his feet and limped a few steps on his burnt feet. "When I was a kid," he said, "my grandad used to play Monopoly with me. He insisted it was great fun, better than any videogame I might find. Of course, I thought it was boring as hell, but my parents insisted I give the old guy a few hours of company each week, so I didn't have much choice. Grandad beat me every time, without fail. He never gave me a chance or handicapped himself, just kept on beating me. The last time we played — the last time before he died — I flipped that goddamn Monopoly board so high it almost hit the ceiling fan. I can still picture the look on my Grandad's face. He was heartbroken. I've never stopped regretting what I did that day. But this day is different."

Leo frowned. "You've lost me, dude."

"What I'm trying to tell you, man, is that this time I will have zero fucking regrets about flipping the board on this goddamn game."

Slowly, a grin crept onto Leo's face and he nodded. "Nice."

"We need to find the next game," said Cheryl.

Leo folded his arms and looked at her. "I thought our whole plan was to *not* play the game."

"It is, but I want to find out what we're *supposed* to do so we can do something else. Let's find the next cell."

After checking on John and Maggie, and still deciding

that nothing could be done, they got to work. It didn't take them long to find what they were looking for. There were only two cells left, and both were unlit, but while one had a padlock the other seemed to have some kind of magnetic bolt on it. The padlock had numbers on the rollers, of which there were only two. Printed above the two rollers were a pair of letters. P and M.

"Polly McIntyre," said Leo, although it was obvious enough, "and two numbers. What combination would only be two numbers?"

"Age," said Monty. "Try putting Polly's age."

Leo looked at Monty and licked his bottom lip. "How old was she? I'm not sure if she was eighteen or nineteen."

"She was eighteen," said Monty. "We had drinks for her birthday a few weeks before she vanished, remember?" He winced and rephrased it. "Before Alfie *buried* her under a shipping container. Fuck."

Alfie lowered his head in shame and said nothing. What *could* he say? They all wanted out of there, but Alfie was facing jail time if they reported his crime, and Cheryl, for one, would *absolutely* report it. It was just a shame Happy wasn't alive to find out what had happened to his niece.

But what was Happy's part in all this? What was his *crime? Which sin did he die for?*

Leo rolled in the number **18** and the padlock instantly popped. He unthreaded it from the gate and pushed it open but didn't step inside. It was still dark. Cheryl waved a hand just inside the gate to capture the sensor's attention. The room lit up like the others. They were presented with something dreadfully recognisable.

A noose.

Behind the noose was a television. White words appeared on a black background.

Polly McIntyre died October 14th 2016 aged 18. She left behind a loving mother, Sharon, and a younger brother, Michael. Her cause of death was strangulation.

Cheryl and Leo looked at one another, then both looked at Alfie. "I thought she died from being run over."

Alfie held his hand sup. "That's what John told me, I swear. She was dead when I got there."

Cheryl glanced back down the tunnel to where John and Maggie were still lying together. She didn't even know if they were still alive. "My God, Polly must have been alive after the accident. John must have strangled her to keep her from getting help."

Monty covered his mouth, then ran his hand up his face and over his head. "I don't think I can take much more of this."

Alfie hobbled backwards, keeping his hands held protectively out in front of him. "I don't know anything about her being strangled."

The words on screen refreshed.

Congratulations for reaching the truth, but not all secrets have yet been brought to life.

The fans are running backwards. Your oxygen will expire in one hour.

Life Demands Life

Cheryl groaned. She couldn't handle any more secrets,

and frankly she didn't care either. Things couldn't get worse, so why keep torturing them? The timbre of the ceiling fans changed, the blades running in the opposite direction. Did that mean the air was actively being sucked out of the tunnel? It might have been her mind playing tricks on her, but she already felt stifled. Her head began to throb.

"What are we supposed to do?" Leo was rubbing at the burns on his hand again. Did he need more Vaseline? She decided it wasn't important.

Monty pinched his forehead, creating vertical wrinkles. "We're supposed to hang ourselves, bruh. What else could a noose mean?"

"I'll go in and take a look around," said Leo with a defeated sigh, but Cheryl grabbed his arm.

"No! We're not playing along anymore, remember?"

"But we're going to suffocate down here if we refuse to do anything."

"Not yet we're not. Let's think of something this psycho doesn't expect."

Alfie folded his arms, burying his hands under his armpits. "So, we should *not* hang ourselves then? Sounds good to me."

Cheryl took a slow walk down the tunnel, looking all around. The bulbs above her head were just out of reach, as were the fan blades now running backwards. She walked past the curtain hiding Happy's fate and past the cell full of half-burnt supplies. There was nothing they could use. Nothing that jumped out at her and filled her with ideas. When she had decided to no longer play along, she'd hoped some magnificent plan would come to her, but nothing came to mind.

Time and oxygen were running out.

John was still alive, mumbling to himself at the front end of the tunnel. Despite the fact she now considered the man a remorseless monster, she couldn't ignore his suffering, so she went over to him. "John, you're still with us?"

He resembled a corpse, grey-skinned and white-lipped. Despite that, his eyes were fully open and he focused on her. "Cheryl... Cheryl, is everyone—"

"No, everyone is not okay, John. We're in a bad way, and it's because of you. This is all happening because of what you did to Polly McIntyre."

He winced, like the mere mention of the name hurt him. He also looked shocked, as if Cheryl had just performed a magic trick. Or shared his deepest secret. "Y-You know?"

"That you then mowed down Happy's niece and covered up her death? Yeah, I know all about that. I know Maggie was with you too, and that you dragged Alfie into it and made him bury Polly's body. Whoever tricked us down here knows too. Someone is punishing you, John. Do you have any idea who?"

He closed his eyes for a second, and she thought he might have fallen back unconscious, but it appeared he had only been thinking because he looked at her again. "Polly's mother? Her brother? Even Happy would want me dead if he knew. It's impossible though. How could anyone know? It was just an accident."

"Then who strangled her, John? How is that an accident?"

He frowned, and with his ashen skin it made him appear even more ghoulish. His words were becoming drawn-out as his energy departed. "W-What are you talking about?"

"Polly was strangled to death."

"No... she wasn't. I hit her. She came out of nowhere and I hit her." A tear escaped down his cheek, but Cheryl could only sneer at him. The judgement seemed to upset him even more. "It was an accident, I'm telling you."

"That you forced Alfie to cover up?"

He turned his head slightly to the side and seemed to be

looking at his nephew who was scouring the other end of the tunnel with Leo and Monty. It was a miracle he was able to stand after being so badly burned. "I panicked. I shouldn't have got him involved. He doesn't deserve to be in this."

"Yes, he does. You all deserve this. Monty's a thief, you're a murderer, Alfie buries bodies. Jeez, even Leo, who I actually started to think was a decent guy, is guilty of blackmailing himself a promotion."

John turned his head back to look at her. "What are you talking about?"

"Leo told me about how he blackmailed you with evidence of you cheating on your wife. I know he forced you to give him a promotion."

"I promoted him because he's good at his job. He... He never blackmailed me."

Cheryl hissed. "No more lies John. The truth is out. I know everything. Every little sin."

"You're wrong. Leo never blackmailed me. My wife wouldn't even care. Karen and I... we haven't..." He blinked and swallowed, almost like he was suddenly confused. "I don't know why Leo lied to you, Cheryl, but he never threatened me. It wouldn't have worked even if he had."

She was about to defend Leo, but somehow she knew what John was saying was the truth. In actual fact, the thought of John allowing Leo to blackmail him seemed absurd. "You're really telling me the truth, John? Because if—"

"I swear it, Cheryl. I'm telling the truth about everything. I hit Polly with Monty's car and covered it up. Why would I lie about anything else?"

"You didn't strangle her?"

"I swear. I deserve this, I know, but it was just an accident that got out of hand. I would never strangle someone to death."

Cheryl believed him. In all the pain and delirium, she didn't think John was even capable of lying anymore. It would be an effort he could not summon. He was dying and he knew it. His confession was real, an attempt to unburden himself. Perhaps he thought the truth might set him free.

So who strangled Polly?

Alfie said Polly had been dead when he'd arrived. If it hadn't been John who'd strangled Polly then it could only have been one other person.

Maggie was still sprawled across John's legs. Cheryl shook the woman. "Mag? Mag, are you still alive? Mag, I need to talk to you." She was certain the woman was still alive because she was hot, burning up in fact. A dead body would be cold, right?

Mag moaned and lifted her head. A long line of mottled saliva hung from her mouth. "C-Cheryl, help me, please."

"I'm trying to, Mag, but I need to know the truth — the truth about Polly McIntyre."

"She's.... She's missing."

"No, she's not, Mag. She's dead, and I know you were involved. You were in the car that hit her."

"Yes." It was a surprise when she didn't try to deny it, but she too was at death's door. The will to lie obviously slipped away when a person neared death.

"Was Polly dead when you found her in the woods?"

Maggie didn't answer.

"Mag, please tell me the truth. Was Polly McIntyre dead when you went to her after the accident? Did John kill her, or something else?"

"Still alive. I... I tried to help while John called for help. She was in a bad, in a bad way, bleeding all over, crying. She kept saying she needed to tell the police, that she needed to tell them what had been done to her. She kept saying it over and over again."

"That she was going to tell the police?"

"Yes! She said *he* was a monster and that she would tell them everything. John was trying to get a signal on his phone, to get her some help, but all she could do was threaten to ruin his life." She blinked her eyes slowly, beginning to fade. The talking was tiring her. "It was an accident. John didn't deserve to go to prison."

"He'd been drinking and doing drugs, and you were... taking care of him in the passenger seat. He had no business being behind the wheel."

Maggie didn't seem to be listening anymore. "I kept telling Polly, it was just an accident, but she wouldn't listen. She kept asking for the police. Kept saying he was a monster. I couldn't let John go down for an accident."

"Or yourself," said Cheryl, "because you strangled her."

"The stupid girl left me, left me no choice. Cheryl, please help, please help, please—" She turned her head and bloody vomit escaped her lips. It covered John's legs, and he reached out to hold her, but he was too weak, almost asleep.

Almost dead.

Maggie, too, looked done for. Her eyes were red, every vessel burst. The liquid coming out of her was foul-smelling and mixed with blood, while the fingers on both hands contorted so badly they threatened to snap. Her neck bulged to twice its size.

"Cheryl, please. Cheryl, please help me, me, me—" She seized again, more blood coming from her mouth, her nose, her eyes.

Her ears.

Maggie slumped forwards over John's lap. She went still.

Cheryl shook her. "Mag? Mag, can you hear me?"

Leo, Alfie, and Monty came rushing over. "Is everything okay?"

Cheryl examined Maggie's face, prodded at her neck and

tried to feel a pulse. Eventually, she had to turn to the others and break the news. "She's dead."

It hit them all equally, and they fell silent. John was still awake, but it was unclear whether or not he understood what had happened. Eventually Leo came and put an arm around Cheryl. She had to force herself not to flinch. If she reacted badly to his touch, he would know something was up. He might sense that she had unanswered questions about him; like why had he lied about blackmailing John?

And what was the real reason he was down there? What was he truly guilty of?

Leo squeezed Cheryl tightly, and she had no choice but to let herself be hugged.

CHAPTER EIGHT

Rather than leave her body sprawled on top of John, Leo and Monty slid Maggie away gently, leaving her beside the dissected TVR. Monty remained there for a while, staring at the car that had once been his. "It really is my old car," he said when Cheryl approached him. "For two years I thought I'd got drunk and wrapped it around a tree. I woke up in my hotel room the next morning, and the police were already waiting for me when I went for breakfast. My uncle the soliciter had taught me never to say anything so I didn't, but it never made much sense. I remembered none of it, and I never had a scratch on me, not even a scrap of dirt. The cops couldn't place me in the car at the time of the accident so they brought no charges, but it didn't stop me from feeling ashamed. I thought I'd driven drunk and almost killed myself."

Cheryl put a hand on his back. "You didn't do anything wrong."

"Yeah, I did. I drank myself unconscious and shamed myself. I'm Muslim. If I'd followed Allah then I would have been sober and alert that night. John wouldn't have got away with everything that he did."

"Look, Monty, I don't give much thought to God, or Allah, but I don't think people are supposed to be perfect. Life is tough, and it just goes on and on whether we like it or not. The only thing we can do is make the best of it and try to be good. You're a good man, Monty. I see it now."

He looked at her and grunted. "We both know that ain't true."

"Perhaps, but you have a choice now. From this very moment, you can be whoever you want to be. If you don't like who you *were* then make sure you like who you'll *become*. It's never too late to start making things right."

Monty looked down at Maggie's puke-stained corpse. "Sometimes it is."

The fact he was beating himself up only reinforced Cheryl's gut feeling that Monty was a good man deep down. He'd bought a little too much into the ruthless world of sales and business, but the truth was that he had screwed people over rather than physically hurt them. And right now he wasn't proud of it.

Could she trust him? Should she tell him that Leo was keeping secrets? Perhaps he would know something she didn't. Before she could open her mouth, Leo approached, holding one of the fallen ladder rungs and the bloody meat cleaver that had taken John's wrist.

"Get that thing away from me," said Monty, grimacing. "Why do you even have it?"

Leo lowered the cleaver next to his thigh, out of eye-line, but he handed the steel rung over to Monty. "Thought we could do with some tools — or weapons maybe. If we start trying to claw our way out of this hole, we might encounter resistance."

"You think so?" Cheryl had only been thinking about

escaping and had paid no consideration to the fact there were people who planned on keeping them trapped. Arming up was a sensible idea but seeing Leo with a bloody meat cleaver in his hand did not fill her with confidence.

Alfie was with John, chatting quietly. Cheryl decided to go and join them. "How's he doing, Alfie?"

Alfie's expression answered for him. "I think he's about to go."

Cheryl knelt down and put an arm around him. Beneath his jacket, Alfie's waist was thinner than hers, and she was surprised to find herself jealous. The petty emotion was somehow comforting after feeling nothing but fear and terror for the last several hours. John appeared to be sleeping, and it even sounded like he was snoring, but the rhythm of his breathing was all wrong.

"Were you close to your uncle, Alfie?" Cheryl asked

Alfie gave a mild smile. "Yeah, I was for a long time; then Polly died and things just got, I dunno, weird. He always looked out for me, and after what happened he kept me even closer, but I think it was just to keep an eye on me, really. He wasn't a good bloke, Cher, I know that. The things Maggie said about him were probably true. John had a way of twisting people in knots and making them do whatever he wanted. My mum always warned me not to trust him, but I could never understand why at first because he always seemed to care about me. When I was a kid, I was shy." He held his stunted hand up to her. "Insecure about this. Kids would make fun of me at school, and when I got older I never wanted to go out. John found out and started dragging me down the pub, trying to get me out of my shell. I hated it at first, but whenever he caught someone whispering about my hand, he would go up and give them hell. After a while I started to feel safe in the pub, and I did come out of my shell. Once that happened, girls started to like me, and other lads would drink with me.

Turned out, people only cared about my hand if I did. If I was confident enough to ignore it, then it stopped being an issue. John gave that confidence to me, and it changed my life. He wasn't a good man, Cher, but I loved him."

She smiled. "I get it. I lost my dad a few years back. He was the centre of my universe, but the truth is he could be moody and selfish, and we always had to do whatever he wanted to do. Sometimes he would go away entire weekends without me and mum. Work, he would call it, but I know it's because he wanted a break from us. He wasn't the best dad in the world, but I loved him. I *still* love him. People aren't perfect, Alfie, and it's okay to love them even if they don't always deserve it."

"I'm really sorry for what I've done, Cher. Facing Happy every day, letting Polly's mum wonder all this time. If we live through this—"

She gave him a gentle nudge. "I know. You don't have to say it."

Monty moved over to join them. "Um, guys? I think, I think he's gone."

Alfie leaned forwards and closed his uncle's eyes. "See you in Hell, *unc*."

Cheryl rubbed his back. "You okay?"

"Yeah, I think I'm passed the point where I can feel any worse. Although, there's nothing I wouldn't do for a pack of fags right now."

Leo chuckled joylessly. "I'd do the same for a beer. You still want to get out of here?"

Alfie nodded. "Time I took responsibility. Polly's mum deserves the truth, and not from whatever psychopath she hired to torture us. She needs to hear me say how sorry I am in person."

"It's never too late," said Monty, giving Cheryl a half-smile, "to start making things right."

"Yeah, okay," said Leo, and he gave a sarcastic hand clap. "That's all really lovely and everything, but are we going to go find a way out of here or what? Because, as I see it, we have about forty-five minutes of air left."

Cheryl got to her feet. "Then we best put our heads together, because I refuse to die down here."

Leo was peering into the cell. "So what's the deal with the noose? How will one of us hanging ourselves achieve anything?"

"Someone is controlling things," said Cheryl. "They know whether we're obeying the rules or not. If we hang ourselves, they'll know."

Monty shrugged. "And then what? Let us go?"

"Maybe."

"Well, screw that," said Alfie. "I'm guilty of a lot of things, but I don't plan on hanging myself."

Monty stepped towards the cell, but Cheryl stopped him. "What are you doing?"

"I'm going to take a look. It's okay, I'll be fine." He moved her back and then passed through the gate. He started looking around, moving cautiously. His hands were trembling, which made it clear how afraid he was.

"You see anything?" asked Leo.

"No. Just the noose."

Cheryl looked upwards. "What's it attached to?"

"Hold on, let me see." The lighting was poor, so Monty stood for a while beneath the noose and tried to trace its source. "It's attached to some kind of pulley, threaded around, like, a metal wheel. Looks like it belongs on a ship's rigging or something."

"Okay," said Cheryl, looking up at the tunnel's ceiling and

seeing a thick conduit running overhead between the final two cells. "It's more than just a noose. It's hooked up to something."

Alfie stumbled suddenly and Leo grabbed him. "You okay, dude?"

"Yeah, I just got lightheaded for a second."

"It's the air," said Cheryl. "I'm feeling lightheaded too. I don't think we have very long left."

Monty cursed under his breath, and then he reached for the noose.

Leo banged on the bars. "Whoa, dude, what are you doing?"

"We need to find out what this does before we suffocate. Just chill, okay?" To everyone's relief, Monty didn't place his head inside the noose. He just yanked on it with both hands.

Clunk clunk clunk.

The noose gave obvious resistance, and Monty had to keep a firm grip on it as he pulled it downward. Out in the tunnel, a metallic grinding sounded overhead, coming from the conduit.

Alfie looked up nervously. "What's happening?"

Cheryl realised her stomach was calm, the situation no longer able to surprise her. "I'm not sure," she said. "Nobody panic."

An ear-piercing whine broke out and caused them all to shudder. It was the wail of a blown speaker, or a megaphone. Eventually the sound softened, giving way to a crackling hiss — and then a voice.

It wasn't the voice of the no-eyed man. It was the voice of a young girl.

A young girl in terror.

153

I need you to come get me. I need help. Sobbing sounds. *Please come. Where are you?* Pause. *He, he, he raped me. He raped me! Please, come. Come now.* Crackling, like a phone breaking up. *Hello! Are you still there? Please come. He left me in the woods. I'm... I'm going to try and find the road. I think I hear a car. Please come get me.*

Alfie's eyes were bulging. "That's Polly's voice!"

Monty let go of the noose and it stayed in place. Overhead, the fans clunked to a stop before starting again. Cheryl could tell by the sound that they were once again running the correct way. "The air is coming back. We did it."

Leo fist-pumped the air, but he didn't seem to have much enthusiasm. "Nice one, Monty. Come on, get on out of there."

Monty started towards the gate. The look on his face was one of clear devastation. "That was Polly the night she disappeared. Did you hear how scared she was? She said she'd been ra—"

Monty lurched forward as something struck him in the back. His eyes went wide and he coughed meekly.

Cheryl reached out to him. "Monty, are you—"

He staggered forward into her arms, trying to reach around to his own back. He was too heavy to hold up, and as he tumbled onto his knees, Cheryl saw a metal spike sticking out of his back. A pathetic moan escaped his lips and he slumped heavily onto his stomach. Blood stained the back of his white shirt around a sharp metal spike.

Cheryl screamed.

Above her, the conduit clunked, and inside the cell the noose rose back to its original position. The fans whirled to a halt once more, then started back up again in the opposite direction. Attached to a metal arm that had swung down from the ceiling and planted a spike in Monty's back was a sign. It read: LIFE DEMANDS A LIFE.

"We tried to cheat," said Alfie, "and this is the punishment."

Leo put a hand to his forehead. "One of us is going to have to hang."

Cheryl pressed her hands into the deep stab wound in Monty's back. It didn't bleed as badly as John's wrist had done, but it was still grim. He was breathing, but unconscious. Cheryl didn't have a clue what to do, or even if there was anything she *could* do. She desperately wanted to keep him alive. "We need to plug the wound. Help me stop this bleeding."

Leo didn't move, except to shake his head. "Cher, there's nothing we can do."

"That's bullshit. We can help him, we can..." She looked at her hands, covered in Monty's blood. He was totally still, completely unmoving. Even if he wasn't dead, he would be soon.

"We have to focus on ourselves," said Leo. "Our air is running out."

Alfie knelt next to Cheryl and placed a hand on Monty's shoulder. Then, he looked up at Leo. "He's still breathing, man. Are you saying we just let him die?"

Leo sighed. "I'm saying we have no choice. He's been stabbed in the back. Are any of us doctors? Surgeons? We try to help him and we'll only end up wasting time better spent trying to save ourselves. We need to get those fans running the other way or find a way out of here before our air runs out."

Alfie stood, wincing as he put weight on his burnt feet.

"You already told me I'd get a pass if I climbed inside that bloody kettle. I ain't hanging myself."

"Well, one of us has to do *something*."

"And I say it's your turn, Leo. Why don't you hang yourself and save us?"

Cheryl was in no mood to deal with an argument, so she stood up and grabbed Alfie's arm then looked him in the eye. "No one is hanging themselves, Alfie, but we *are* going to solve this together."

He nodded, taken aback by the force in her voice. "Yeah, okay."

"I agree," said Leo. "I'm not going to stand here and watch one of you die, but we do need to come up with a plan or else we're *all* dead. I would do anything I could to help Monty if there were a way, but there isn't."

Cheryl knew it was true. They couldn't help Monty. "We find a way out of here," she said, "and then we get help. Maybe Monty will last long enough for it to arrive."

Alfie nodded, but it didn't seem like he believed her. "Okay, how are we going to get the fans back on?"

"Maybe I can just go and pull on it," said Leo, "like Monty did."

Alfie shook his head. "It won't work. The reason the fans reversed again is because the noose went back up into the ceiling after Monty let go. It's what triggered the spike to swing down and stab him."

Leo folded his arms. "So to keep the fans running the right way, we need to keep the noose weighted down permanently?"

"With a body," said Cheryl. She stared at the opposite end of the steel tunnel. "We have bodies to spare."

Leo curled his lip in disgust. "Are you serious?"

"Horrifically, yes I am. The noose needs to be weighted down by a body. A body that isn't going to go anywhere."

Alfie started limping away. "I'll get John's legs. Somebody want to help me with his head?"

"I will," said Cheryl, but Leo squeezed her arm gently to keep her from rushing off.

"I'll do it. John is going to be heavy."

"Okay, well, I'm sure we'll manage between the three of us."

In a grim procession, they walked over to John's cooling corpse. Leo let out a yawn that infected the others, and soon they were all covering their mouths like they were stuck at church. The thinning air was sapping the life out of them. They had to move quickly.

Alfie knelt in front of his uncle and placed a hand around his ankle. "I'm sorry, Uncle John. I guess you had it coming though, huh?"

Leo put one of his hands on John's shoulders. He looked at Alfie. "You ready, dude?"

Alfie nodded, and together they hoisted John upwards. The gristly strands holding his severed hand to his wrist finally snapped and the appendage splatted against the ground. Leo used the side of his shoe to kick it to one side. Somehow, it didn't disturb them. It had become normal.

Cheryl didn't lift John, but she walked between Alfie and Leo, ready to help if needed. She detected a musky odour and realised John had wet himself at some point, maybe even after he died. The flesh of his face seemed to sag, making him look older and greyer. It didn't seem like John at all.

They all moved to the other end of the tunnel, then slowed in front of the cell with the noose.

"How we going to get him up?" Leo asked.

"We might all have to lift him together," said Alfie.

Leo moved into the cell first, taking John's head end with him. Alfie hooked his uncle's feet beneath his armpits and tottered after him. Cheryl felt weak. Tired.

"Help me get him up," said Leo, starting to lift John's body. Alfie wrapped an arm around his uncle's waist and hoisted. Cheryl placed a hand on John's sweaty, dead back to keep him steady. Leo groaned. "Push. I'm dropping him, I'm dropping—"

John's body began to tilt, but Cheryl switched her grip and managed to shove him the other way. At the same time, Alfie hoisted John around the middle. There was a thickening crunch as the noose caught around John's neck and crunched the fragile bones inside. The flesh beneath his chin bulged, making him look bloated.

"Okay," said Leo. "Step back."

Alfie hobbled away, hissing with every step.

John's sagging corpse swung from its neck. The sight was horrifying. Lynching even a dead body was sickening, and it disturbed her that people used to gather in public to watch people hang.

The noose began to lower, inch-by-inch. They waited for the sound of the fan blades changing direction. *Clunk, clunk, whir.*

Cheryl staggered out of the cell and called to Monty, hoping he would answer her and tell her that he was fine, but he didn't. Suddenly tired, she eased herself down to the ground to rest. It might have been in her head, but after a few minutes, her sluggish, dazed feeling went away.

"I think we did it," said Leo, joining her on the ground. He placed a hand on her back and she shifted away, more forcefully than she'd intended. Clearly, he noticed it. "Hey, what's up, Cher-bear? Everything okay?"

"Yeah, just, um, feeling a bit jumpy." *Especially around liars. What did you do Leo? If you never blackmailed John, what did you do?*

Did you rape Polly?

Alfie stood outside the cell, staring in at his dead Uncle.

Cheryl could only imagine what was going through his head right now. Poor kid. His uncle had really dragged him into a nightmare. The last two years must have been horrible, constantly waiting for someone to find Polly's body and for the police to tie everything together. Now, even if he got out of here, Alfie's life was over.

Leo reached out and put his hand on Cheryl's back again. This time she forced herself to endure it. "We're almost there," he said. "We're nearly out of this hole, Cher, I know it."

She smiled and hoped she didn't look too nervous. "I hope you're right."

"Maybe there's still a chance I'll get to take you out for a night on the town. Surviving a torture chamber brings people closer together, right?"

She tittered, wondering how he could joke so easily. Monty, Happy, John, and Maggie were all dead, and he was still focusing on getting her out on a date. With her best effort, she tried to chuckle. "Ha, yeah, so um, we should start looking for a way out of here now that we're not in imminent danger of suffocating."

Leo frowned as she once again slipped out of his grasp. She hopped up and brushed herself down, before going and standing next to Alfie who was still staring through the bars at his uncle. "Alfie, I'm really sorry. You must be in pain." *Physically and emotionally.*

"Not as much as I deserve," he told her, and didn't seem upset. He seemed defiant. "I'm ready for the last cell."

"The last—" Cheryl turned and realised what he was referring to. There was one cell remaining. One cell with a magnetic bolt that had now slid aside. It was unlocked.

The final game had begun.

CHAPTER NINE

CHERYL'S CURIOSITY lit a fire beneath her, making her arrive in front of the cell before Leo and Alfie had a chance to get there. As soon as she touched the gate, the interior lit up. The last thing she'd expected to find was a sofa and television. The cell almost resembled a lounge, only with steel walls, floor, and ceiling.

"Looks like it's movie time," said Leo.

Alfie moved slowly inside and sat down on the right side of the sofa, tucking the steel rung Leo had given him down the side of the cushion. Cheryl wished he'd sat in the middle so that she could avoid sitting next to Leo, but as it was, Leo sat on the left, leaving Cheryl no option but to plonk herself down in the middle. There was no evidence Leo had even done anything, but the seed of doubt had been planted in her mind and was beginning to sprout. The fact he sat right next to her with a bloody cleaver laying across his lap didn't help matters.

Cheryl felt something click underneath the cushion as she settled back. The television flashed to life. Their old friend appeared, the man with no eyes. He was smiling.

"The road through perdition is at an end. Will you now pass into the light of atonement, or sink forever into the Abyss? One crime still lies uncovered in the reeking undergrowth. See it uncovered."

The screen went black momentarily before a new scene played. It looked like footage from a hidden camera, the view partially obscured by something blocking the lens. Cheryl recognised the location almost immediately. It was John's office. The camera was filming from the bookshelf behind the desk.

"It's a spy camera," said Leo. "In John's office."

Alfie leant forward on the sofa. "Who put it there?"

Cheryl shushed them both. On screen, John and Maggie were walking into the office.

"You still on for tonight?" Maggie asked John.

John moved behind his desk, almost like he was trying to put a barrier between them. "Maybe it's not such a good idea, Mag. We had our fun, but let's not get our fingers burned. You want Andrew finding out?"

"I don't care. I didn't think you did either. You were the one that popped round to share a beer with him."

"That was before..."

"Before what? Before I helped you cover up a murder?"

"It was an accident," said John. "And will you keep your voice down? I just think that with all that has happened, we should let things cool off. I've had enough excitement to last me a lifetime. Haven't you?"

Maggie slunk around his desk and cornered him. She used her fingertips to ride up her skirt and pressed herself against John. "Oh, come on! The thing you need most right now is a little," she grabbed his cock, "stress-relief. All the bad stuff is behind us. The police have stopped asking questions. Polly McIntyre will remain an unsolved mystery thanks to your nephew."

"We should never have dragged Alfie into this."

She kept rubbing at his cock, getting a rise out of him. He didn't try to stop her. "You were the one who got him involved, John. It can't be helped now." She dropped to her knees, only the top of her head now visible on camera.

On the sofa, Alfie groaned. "Seriously, I don't need to see this."

John grabbed Maggie's shoulders and yanked her back to her feet. "I don't want this, Maggie. We've fucked up enough people's lives without ruining our marriages as well. Just back off."

Maggie snarled like a feral cat. She glared at John, her face only inches from his. "You think you can fuck me when it suits you, then toss me aside once you're bored? Is that it? I tried to break it off with you, and you weren't having it. Now you decide you're done and I'm just supposed to accept it, huh?"

"No, that's not it. I care about you, Maggie, but I need space right now. Perhaps you should go work some place else."

Maggie lunged at John, poking him right in the centre of the chest. "Try and get rid of me, I dare you. I'm not going anywhere, John. You owe me."

John perched back on his desk and sighed. "I know I do, Mag. I'm just all over the place. I don't want anybody else getting hurt."

Maggie's mood changed back to sultry. She slid a hand inside his shirt. "Then stop making drama where there is none. It's okay to be happy, John — even after what happened."

"What we did."

"What *you* did, John. You were driving the car. The only reason I covered for you is because I love you."

He sighed. "I love you too. I'm sorry I dragged you into this mess."

"It's all behind us now. Stop worrying."

They kissed.

The screen went blank.

Alfie snorted derisively. "I knew Maggie was a few crackers short of a hamper, but I didn't know she was a full on lunatic."

"They both seemed as bad as each other to me," said Leo.

"And they're both dead," said Cheryl, deciding she didn't want to insult the departed, if only because it was a waste of breath. "Who placed a camera in John's office?"

"Beats me," said Alfie. "He couldn't have known it was there."

"Maybe he was making sex tapes of Maggie," said Leo. "Wouldn't put it past him."

Cheryl didn't think so somehow. "It didn't seem like John had any idea he was being filmed. The camera was hidden in his bookcase."

"And he never touched the books," said Leo. "They were all there for show."

Alfie chuckled. "Yeah, he bought a load of old Dickens novels on eBay and told people he had spent years collecting them. He was such a flash git."

I need you to come get me. I need help.

Everyone looked around. It was Polly's voice again, the same recording they'd heard earlier. It was coming from above them, and maybe even from out in the tunnel too.

Please come. Where are you? Pause. *He-he-he... He raped me. He raped me! Please, come. Come now.* Crackling, like a phone breaking up. *Hello! Are you still there? Please come. He left me in the woods. I'm... I'm going to try and find the road. I think I can hear a car. Please come.*

This time the recording didn't stop. A man's voice replied

to Polly's, but it was electronically distorted to hide its identity. *Who raped you?*

Leo! It was Leo!

Alfie leapt up off the sofa. He stared at Leo, stunned. "What the fuck, man?"

Cheryl scooted along the sofa to get distance between her and Leo. She dared not get up in case he grabbed her. "I knew it! God, I knew it."

Leo stood up. He raised his eyebrows at them, a bemused blend of panic and confusion on his face. "Come on, guys, what the hell? I didn't rape Polly. It's fucking ridiculous. I'm being set up."

Alfie backed up against the bars and pointed a finger at Leo. "You went after her that night, man. She had a blazing row with Monty in the hotel bar, then went outside looking for John. She said she had something to tell him."

"Yeah, I went after her," said Leo, shrugging like it was no great admission. "She was in a right state. Monty really let her have it."

Cheryl tried to consolidate the Leo she knew with a rapist and found it difficult. As much as she had suspected something, this was a shock. "What was Polly upset about?"

Leo shrugged. "I dunno."

"Bullshit," said Alfie. "You set off right after she did. No way you wouldn't have caught up to her. What did she tell you?"

"Okay, fine! She said Monty stole the council deal from her. It was *her* lead, one she had been working on for months. The order finally came through, but Monty said he had closed it himself because she would have lost it if he hadn't."

Alfie cursed. "That piece of shit. He's been stealing sales for years. He must have logged into the system and stolen the contact details Polly had set up. That's why they had a blazing row at the bar. She must have confronted him."

"No wonder they thought Monty had something to do with her disappearance," said Cheryl. "He must have seemed guilty as hell after arguing with her in the bar."

"But it had nothing to do with him," said Alfie. "John killed her and I buried her."

"Actually," said Cheryl. "It was Maggie who killed her. She admitted it to me right before she died. Polly was still alive after John hit her."

Alfie looked like he was going to be sick. He covered his mouth with both hands. "We're all monsters."

"Speak for yourselves," said Cheryl.

"I haven't done anything either," Leo protested. He looked so utterly mortified that she began to wonder if he might be innocent. But Polly herself had named him.

Cheryl turned to Alfie, got up and moved over to him. "How long was there between Leo chasing after Polly and John texting you to meet him at the pond?"

"I suppose about forty-minutes. Definitely less than an hour. The walk to where she got hit was about ten minutes."

Cheryl turned her stare on Leo as she did the math. "That leaves thirty minutes unaccounted for. What happened to cause Polly to take forty minutes making a ten minute walk?"

Leo shrugged. "She wanted to go for a walk and clear her head. I spoke to her for a while and then left her alone. I went back to the hotel."

"You're a goddamn liar," said Alfie. He pointed in Leo's face again. "You never came back that night. I stayed outside smoking with one of the barmaids who knocked off at eleven. I never saw you again until morning. You were loaded, and you had a thing for Polly. You went after her and you fucking raped her, didn't you?"

"I didn't, you moron."

"Yes, you did! We all heard Polly's voice on that recording. She phoned somebody. Somebody who has known all along what we did to her. This is their revenge, and we deserve it, but you most of all. If you hadn't chased after Polly and attacked her, she never would have run out into the road. John wouldn't have hit her and made us all cover it up. All of this has happened because of you, you sick piece of shit. You ruined our lives, Leo."

Cheryl yelped as Alfie pushed her down on the sofa so that he could launch himself at Leo. Leo leapt backwards but found himself trapped up against the wall. Terrified, he threw up his hands blindly in front of himself.

And buried the cleaver right in Alfie's neck.

There was a quick spurt of blood, and then nothing but stillness and silence. Alfie stood in front of Leo, frozen solid, while Leo stared into his eyes with a look of shock. Gradually, Alfie's body slackened. His one arm hung so limply, it almost made it to his knees. He managed to bring up his other hand — his stunted hand — and attempted to pull the cleaver out of his neck. It wasn't buried too deep. There wasn't much blood. Maybe he would be all right.

With a glazed look of madness in his eyes, Leo pulled the cleaver free from Alfie's neck. He mumbled words, apologies and excuses, and then buried the cleaver again, deeper into the open wound. Blood spat from Alfie's mouth and he tried to say something, but Leo pulled the cleaver free again and silenced him.

Alfie collapsed backwards onto the sofa, legs flopping over the armrest. Cheryl screamed. In her mind, she had been running away and trying to get help, but in reality she hadn't moved an inch. She had stood beside the sofa and watched the entire thing. She had watched Leo murder Alfie in cold blood.

And now she was alone with a killer.

Cheryl moved towards the gate. Leo stumbled after her. He had just murdered Alfie, but he acted as though it had been an accident. "Cher, come on, please, just let me talk. I can explain."

"Okay, Leo, just don't hurt me."

"Hurt you? Cher-bear, that's the last thing I want. I really like you."

"In the same way you liked Polly?" Cheryl didn't know why she asked such an antagonising question, it had just spilled out of her. Anger spilled out of her. "Are you going to rape me like you raped her?"

He moved towards her, waving the bloody cleaver around like he forgot he was even holding it. It sliced back and forth through the air, flicking Alfie's blood at her. "I didn't rape Polly! How could you think that?"

"I heard the recording, Leo. Polly was pretty clear about who had hurt her."

"She's a fucking liar. We were all drunk that night, Cher, but Polly had a chip on her shoulder about something from the moment she arrived. She was determined to have a good time and made no secret of it. We were making out in the bar well before she got into a row with Monty. I only went after her to continue what we'd started. She wanted it."

Cheryl shook her head in disgust. "Making out with someone in a bar doesn't mean they want to get fucked in the woods."

Leo pointed the cleaver at her. "She wanted it."

"Let me out of this cell, Leo."

"Not until you say you believe me."

Seriously? He was waving a meat cleaver at her that he had just used to murder Alfie. Did it really matter whether she believed him or not? "Okay, I believe you, Leo. Please, step out of my way."

To her astonishment he did as she asked and stepped out

of her way so that she could make it to the gate clear. She hurried and, when Leo made a move to follow, she panicked. She leapt through the gate and turned to swing it shut. The metal frame struck Leo and trapped his arm against the bars.

"You stupid bitch!"

"Leo, stay back or I swear—"

"Swear what? You're just like all the others, Cheryl. Giving guys the come on when it suits you then cock-blocking once it's time to deliver. I've been nothing but nice to you, and you're treating me like an arsehole."

"You murdered Alfie."

"It was an accident."

Leo threw the cell gate open and approached her in the centre of the tunnel. He had the look of a wild dog, tensed up and ready to bite. Cheryl's heart beat against her chest, trapped inside her ribs the same way she was trapped inside this tunnel. There was nowhere to run. No escape. She was at the mercy of a monster.

"Help!" she screamed, hoping whoever was listening — if anybody was — would hear her and finally put a stop to this. She wasn't supposed to be down there. This wasn't her game. "Help me, please!

Leo grabbed her and threw her sideways against the steel wall of the tunnel. She struck the back of her head and a few seconds passed without her knowledge. Suddenly Leo was pressed up against her, the bloody cleaver flat against the side of her face. She felt the heat of his groin against hers. "Are you in on this?" he said, snarling the words at her. "Is that why you joined Alscon? To mess everything up for everyone? Who are you, Cheryl?"

She wanted to fight her way free, but she didn't want him to chase her again. Somehow being chased was worse than being caught. "What are you talking about, Leo? None of this has anything to do with me. I'm not even supposed to be here."

"But you are. You're here, and you're fucking everything up. Sticking your nose into other people's business."

She actually grinned at that. "You idiot. Someone has had your number this whole time. You're not as smart as you think you are. This has been one big set up and you fell for it. You're getting what you deserve. Everyone here helped kill Polly, but what you did is by far the worst. Leo, you're the monster down here, buried beneath the earth. This is all because of you." She sneered at him, enjoying the offence it caused. "And you're screwed."

The anger that flashed across his face was terrifying. He lashed out with the cleaver, smacking her in the side on the head with the flat of the blade. She tried to stay on her feet, but the floor tilted and she suddenly found herself on her hands and knees, scurrying to get away. Leo dropped onto her back, pinning her to the ground. Right away she felt his fingers clawing at the waist band of her jeans. "If I'm so screwed then I have nothing to lose, right? Might as well enjoy myself. Looks like you're about to get screwed too."

Cheryl tried to claw herself from underneath him, but his weight crushed her against the steel floor. "Leo, please, don't do this. Get off me!"

Leo panted at the back of her neck. "That's just what Polly said, and you know how things ended for her."

"Get off me!" She threw her head back and felt something crunch. Leo cried in pain and half-climbed away from her.

"You bitch!"

Cheryl tried to scramble away, but Leo grabbed her pony-tail and yanked her head back. Then he smashed her face into the steel floor. She groaned, seeing stars, and the fight went out of her. Leo allowed her to roll onto her side so that she could see what she had done. His nose dripped blood onto her chest. Her head had connected with his nose, and the crimson mask covering his mouth and chin made him look demonic. "I'm really sorry things didn't work out between us, Cher. I always had hope we would make a go of things."

Cheryl groaned through the pain in her head. If this was the manner of her death, she wasn't going to lie there and accept it. "You... never... had... a chance."

Leo cursed and punched her in the face. Cheryl's head whipped to one side and her vision swirled. A glint of steel caught her eye. The cleaver was lying on the floor next to Leo's knee. He had placed it down in order to manhandle her. She looked up at him with tears and blood on her cheeks, and while he clearly enjoyed the sight of her misery, it made him blind to the fact she was secretly reaching out a hand towards the cleaver.

"I didn't mean to hurt, Polly," he said as he sat on top of her. He sounded so normal, almost like he truly did regret his crimes. It was only his eyes that gave him away. They were such a dark brown that they almost appeared black in the low light. Evil eyes. How had she never noticed? "I honestly thought she liked me — I think she *did* in a way — but her mood turned after her fight with Monty. She started calling me names and telling me to get away from her. I just lost it. I can't stand women drinking, it turns them into slags, but right then and there I wanted her anyway. After it was over, she kept threatening to accuse me of assaulting her. I knew I had to kill her, but... well, I'm no killer, Cher. I struggled with it, I really did, and that gave the bitch time to break free and leg it into the woods. It was so dark out there that she vanished like a ghost. I chased her in every direction, and just as I found her, she ran out into the road and John smashed her to bits with Monty's car. It was like a gift from God. Polly was never going to tell a soul about what happened now, and John took care of making her disappear. I went to my hotel room and had myself another couple beers from the mini-bar. It was a good night."

Cheryl inched her fingertips towards the cleaver, almost there. "You're sick," she said. "Mentally ill."

"Yeah, maybe. I take after my mum in that respect. She was nutty as a fruit cake. Used to turn up at my high school in her dressing gown. I begged to live with my dad, but he didn't give a shit, so I was stuck with my lunatic mother while she shagged every no mark Tom, Dick, and Harry to get a bit of beer money. I have a goddamn right to be mentally ill, Cher. Hey, maybe that can be my defence if I ever get out of this hole."

"You won't. We're all going to die down here. But you first!" She stretched for the cleaver, ready to grab it and bury it in Leo's neck the same way he had Alfie's.

"Nice try." Leo grabbed the cleaver just as her fingers began to wrap around it. He had seen her going for it — had known the entire time. "Maybe I should chop off a hand to keep you from struggling."

Cheryl screamed in terror as Leo raised the cleaver over his head with a maniacal glint in his eye. His angular face was unkind in every way, a beast pretending to be a man.

I'm going to die down here.

Cheryl jolted and her lungs squeezed out a hollering wail. The weight on her chest increased, and Leo's face pressed right up against hers, eyes open and staring into hers.

Then he flew backwards, removing himself from on top of her.

Cheryl rolled on to her tummy and started crawling away. She was confused when she realised she still had both hands, fingers all still accounted for. Why hadn't Leo cut her? Had he missed? She glanced over her shoulder and saw Leo struggling. Somebody was fighting with him.

"The fuck you doing, bruh? You crazy?"

Cheryl couldn't believe her eyes. Monty grabbed Leo and restrained him. He wasn't dead yet and had regained consciousness. His skin was pale, and he was visibly disorientated, but he had known enough to protect Cheryl. "He's the one, Monty. Leo raped Polly. He killed Alfie."

Monty's face turned to horror. He snarled at Leo who was struggling to break free. "You piece of filth. I'm gonna mash you up!"

Leo tried to get his arms up, but Monty — far larger— scooped him into an arm lock and slammed him face first into the nearest cell bars. The thunk of Leo's skull was sickening and satisfying. He cried out for mercy. "She's lying, man. I never did nothing. She's in on this whole thing. Don't you think it's weird how she only just started at Alscon? She helped set us up."

Cheryl shook her head because she feared Monty was considering the question seriously. "He raped Polly, I swear," she cried. "It was right after you and she had an argument in the bar. She said you stole her sale to the council. Leo went right after her."

Monty frowned, obviously confused after having just roused from unconsciousness. His back was covered in blood, and the spike was lying on the ground.

Leo relaxed, keeping a non-threatening and easy-going expression on his face. "Nah, man, she's lying. You know me, Monty. I wouldn't hurt a fly."

Leo started to remove himself from Monty's grasp, obviously feeling he had gained enough trust. Monty twisted his arm again and shoved him back against the bars. "You did leave right after Polly. I remember telling the police that but they had a hard on for me being the guilty one. I thought I was guilty, too, because it was me that made her rush off looking for John. If I hadn't stolen her sale..."

Cheryl saw the anguish Monty carried inside him. The

arrogant salesman act had fallen away completely now and his soft underbelly was exposed. "Monty," she said softly, "you're the only one who didn't contribute to Polly's death — not really. You and she had an argument, sure, but if Leo hadn't attacked her, and if John hadn't been speeding around drunk and high, Polly would still be alive. The worst you deserve is getting fired. You deserve a second chance."

Monty looked at her, trembling as he restrained Leo against the bars. He gave Cheryl a small nod, as though she had just spoken words he had longed to hear. He opened his mouth to speak, but then he glanced aside and spotted John hanging from a noose — a decision they had made without him. "What the hell?"

Leo took advantage of the distraction and twisted out of Monty's grasp. Monty reacted and went to grab him again, but Leo circled his arms into a bear hug and squeezed. He clawed at the gaping wound in Monty's back.

Monty bellowed in agony and slumped up against the bars. Leo didn't waste a second. He smashed a knee into Monty's ribs and sent him sprawling onto his stomach. Then he reached down and retrieved the fallen cleaver. Why hadn't Cheryl thought to grab it?

Why didn't I do something?

Leo knelt on Monty's back, pinning him to the ground. "Sorry about this, bruh, but I'm done playing games." He pounded the cleaver into the back of Monty's skull. Again and again and again.

Leo tried to yank the cleaver back out of Monty's skull, but it was embedded too deeply. It was buried almost up to the hilt, and the first blow had shut Monty off like a switch. After somehow surviving being impaled in the back, Monty had been murdered by someone he had trusted. Once again, Cheryl was alone with Leo.

But at least he's no longer armed.

That still doesn't mean there's anywhere to run.

"Leo, you have to stop this. You're out of control."

Leo chuckled. The blood on his chin was now drying, making it darker and even more unsettling. He waved a bloody hand in the air making a 'loopy' gesture. "We lost control the moment we climbed into this hole. We were dead the minute that ladder fell apart in my hands. Isn't it a head fuck?"

"You're right, Leo, and if you kill me you'll be all alone down here until however long it takes for you to starve."

"Maybe. Or maybe your dear old mum will get worried and call the police. Help might come and pull me out of here in the knick of time. If you're alive, you'll start telling tales, but if everyone is dead, I can tell the police about how this was all some sick, twisted game that only I survived. It's the only chance I have, don't you reckon?"

Cheryl nodded. Leo was talking sense — from *his* perspective — which meant he knew what he was doing. He wasn't mad. He wasn't deluded. He was remorseless. A sociopath who had been working in the cubicle next to hers for three months. While Polly's murder had taken a toll on the others, Leo didn't seem to care one bit. In fact, he thought he was the victim in all this.

He took a step towards her. Cheryl stepped back.

"Make it easier on yourself, Cher-bear. We can have some fun before I, you know—" He ran a finger across his throat and made an *ick-ick* sound.

"Stay away from me, you sick bastard."

Leo smirked and took another step. Cheryl took another step back. Slowly, he was chasing her down the tunnel. He seemed to enjoy her defiance, but eventually she would run out of tunnel.

Leo took another step. Cheryl took another step, but this time it was to meet him. Her approach confused him, and it made him reach out to grab her. While he was unbalanced, she swung her foot up between his legs as hard as she could. Once again, she wished she was wearing boots.

All of the air escaped Leo in a massive *ooph*. He toppled over like a wheelbarrow, knees pressed together and his hands covering his battered groin. Cheryl knew she had to keep on attacking if she had any chance, so she rushed forwards and kicked Leo again, this time on top of his head. The blow stung her foot, but she kept on attacking, stamping on him, and booting at his body until he withered into a fetal position. The puppy-like whimpers he made were music to her ears. She stopped fearing him and felt only disgust. "You're what makes my mum so afraid. It's men like you that make women fear every dark alley and lonely pathway, but actually you're not even a man. You're a sad—" She kicked him again. "Pathetic—" And again. "Little—" And again. "B—"

Leo threw out a hand and caught her leg. It knocked her off balance and she stumbled onto one knee. Desperate to keep her attacker off his feet, she leapt at him, pummelling his ears with both hands. But it was no good.

Leo shoved her away. He remained bent, still in pain from the blow to his testicles, but it only seemed to piss him off. Whatever anger had possessed him before, now became an unbridled fury. He lunged at Cheryl with both hands clenched, spittle flying from his mouth as he hissed and snorted.

Cheryl tried to clamber away, letting out a sequel of fear. She tried to defend herself.

But it was over.

She was a defenceless young girl at the mercy of a hungry man. A story as old as time itself.

Leo grabbed her arm and prepared to beat her, but she didn't cower. She would put up whatever fight she had left in her. Men might be bigger than women, but they weren't stronger.

Leo reached for her neck, and Cheryl glared, offering the only defiance she could. She would bite and scratch, spit and swear, but that was only once the beating had begun. This was the moment before. The moment where she foresaw her approaching death, floating through the mist towards her.

Had Polly known her death was coming that night?

Was she as frightened as I am?

Will I see my dad again? Is he watching?

I hope not.

Cheryl collapsed onto her back, her feet kicking at the floor as her throat constricted in Leo's hands.

She began to choke. She began to die.

But then she was weightless, traveling backwards along the ground. She let out a scream, proud that it wasn't completely fearful. Part of the sound was angry. Furious. She continued travelling backwards, something tugging at her shoulders and dragging her. Leo fell away. He knelt on the floor, clutching his forehead. Swearing.

A gate slammed shut, bars rattling, and when Cheryl blinked her eyes she realised that a cell door now separated her from Leo. He glared at her through the bars but seemed shocked by something.

"It's okay," said Happy, grabbing her from behind. "He can't get you in here."

CHAPTER TEN

Happy had to put a hand over Cheryl's mouth to keep her from screaming, but it only made her want to scream more. Having her mouth covered was stopping her from breathing. Happy released her and stepped away. The room was covered in sand, almost like a beach. She sank into it almost to her knees.

"I'm sorry," said Happy. "You were never supposed to be here, but when you turned up, I panicked and saw no other option but to go through with everything. There was too much planning to throw it all away. It was wrong of me."

Leo beat at the bars and bellowed threats at them. Happy yanked the curtain back into place. The curtain that had unfurled after he had apparently suffocated to death.

But he was alive.

"Happy, you're supposed to be dead."

"*Supposed* to be? That's a little unkind, Cheryl. I hope you meant you *thought* I was dead, which is understandable seeing as that was the entire point. As soon as the curtain fell, I escaped the sand."

"Why? I don't understand. What's going on?"

"Revenge," he said with a certain, frightening relish. "Revenge on the people who raped and cheated my innocent, dear niece. Revenge on those who took Polly from us."

Cheryl stared at the curtain, wondering what Leo was doing behind it. Was he trying to find a way inside? There was no doubt. "Happy, why did you do all this?"

"Because Justice demands it. All men deserve a chance to atone before they are judged. What better way to prepare them for their fates."

"You've killed everyone, Happy. They're all dead."

"I did not kill them. In fact, no one needed to die today. Two years have passed since Polly's death. Two years in which any one of them could have come forward and admitted what they had done. Instead, they watched my sister suffer on national TV, and they worked beside me every day without batting an eyelid. I told you John and I were different. Well, it's true. John has always been a monster. His first wife was my sister, and I stayed close to make sure he didn't stray or abuse her. That's why I helped him set up Alscon. Of course he did stray and he did abuse, but I made sure to get evidence. My sister got away just in time to find happiness elsewhere with a daughter."

Cheryl's eyes went wide. "Polly was John's daughter?"

Happy chuckled. "No, not in the slightest. My sister had Polly three years after her divorce, but by then I had already invested too much in Alscon to walk away from John. I didn't see why I should have to. I own a third of it, after all. Well, *all of it* once I pay off John's wife. She's happy to be rid of him too."

Cheryl shook her head in disbelief. "John's wife knew about the affair, just like Andrew did? The three of you planned all this together?"

"No, Cheryl. Justice took care of all of this."

It made no sense at all. If Happy knew what had

happened to Polly, then why hadn't he told the police? Why had he been a part of all this? Why had he come down into this hole with them?

"You're confused, Cheryl, I can tell. Obviously I knew Leo raped my niece the whole time. She called me that night, you heard it yourself. I tried to reach her, to get to her in time, but all I found was John and Maggie, standing beside Monty's crashed TVR. I knew they were involved somehow, but I had no proof. Neither did the police. They couldn't find Polly's body and they had no solid evidence to lead them to anyone. My sister went on the news every chance she got, but eventually the investigation was closed. That was when Justice made an offer. We were asked a simple question: *do you want to know the truth?*"

Cheryl shuffled back on her butt, not wanting to be too close to Happy as he ranted on like a madman. "What are you talking about?"

"I am talking about the man who offered my sister and I closure when nobody else could. Justice placed secret cameras in Alscon and had people begin following the staff. The cameras caught snippets of guilty confessions between John and Maggie, and the whole thing unravelled. A couple of months after the investigation began, Alfie even led us right to Polly's body. Tomorrow, the police will get a tipoff about that container in the woods and she will finally get the resting place she deserves. By then, all those who are guilty will be missing. The evidence of their crimes left behind."

Cheryl was starting to see the bigger picture. "You have recordings of everything that's happened down here?"

Happy tapped the large badge on his lapel. *NEVER GIVE UP.* "I've been filming the close-ups, but there are also cameras in the TVR's headlights and placed inside the light bulbs in the tunnel. There are parabolic mics hidden all over the place. Everything shall be edited appropriately and given to the police. The world will know about the monsters of Alscon, yet no one will ever find their bodies."

Cheryl began to sob. "My mum will wonder where I am. Don't let me disappear."

He reached out and put a hand on her shoulder. "Cheryl, my dear, you're innocent of all this. No one is going to hurt you. Honestly, I'm not sure what to do with you, but you're not guilty like the rest of them."

She swallowed. "Why all these games, Happy? Surely, you could have got a confession some other way?"

"Like I said, all men deserve a chance to atone. If the others had played by the rules of the game and done as asked, they would've been let out eventually. There has to be fairness for Justice to exist, and it was made very clear that John and the others might end up walking away from this scot free." Happy grinned unkindly. "But I knew them all well enough to know they would lie and cheat and turn on one another."

"Monty was sorry," she said, not knowing why she felt any urge to defend him right now. Maybe she was trying to make Happy feel some degree of guilt — to check that he was human. "He screwed Polly over a sale, I know, but he never—"

"Monty's behaviour caught up to him," said Happy. "If you hurt people on purpose, you can't complain about the damage. Trust me, Cheryl, he deserved this as much as any of them. He betrayed Polly. They all did."

There was a loud racket behind the curtain. Cheryl realised Leo was throwing himself against the bars, trying to get in. "I don't know what the hell is going on, Happy, but you're a dead man as soon as I get in there. A dead man."

Happy rolled his eyes. "That burke has no idea."

"No idea about what?"

"There was one person who was not getting out of here alive no matter what. My sister was allowed to pick one person to condemn to certain death. Of course, there was no choice. Leo is past the point of atonement. His death was promised.

"How do we get out of here, Happy? I just want to go home."

He glanced upwards at the hole in the ceiling. "There's a hatch up there. A secret exit meant for me. I was supposed to climb out of here as soon as the curtain drew and concealed me. The perspex container popped open just in time for me to escape and catch my breath, but I wanted to stick around and see how things ended. I deserved that."

Cheryl peered around and noticed that two sides of the perspex container had slid aside to allow the sand to collapse away from Happy and fill the room. It must have been a terrifying experience, even planned. What if Happy's co-conspirators had left him trapped and suffocating? What if something had gone wrong, or they were too late? The focus he must have had on seeing this through was terrifying.

"This is wrong, Happy. You should've gone to the police. You don't have the right to murder people."

"The police had their chance. As for having the right — an eye for the eye, isn't that what they say? Polly's life gave me the right."

Cheryl backed away a little more, shuffling on her butt. This wasn't the Happy she knew, not the kindly old office manager who tacked motivational posters to the walls. He was fragile and cracked, like a crystal statue teetering on a cement ledge. A mild wind might knock him right over to shatter on the ground. Happy had orchestrated the murder of six people — and seemed overjoyed about it.

He obviously saw her trepidation, because he reached out a hand to her again. "Cheryl, it really is okay. It's over. You're safe."

Despite his words, Cheryl flinched and shuffled backwards some more. She wasn't sure why she didn't get to her feet, but the thought of doing so made her feel vulnerable. Sitting on her butt, facing him, nothing could surprise her.

The curtain startled her as she moved into it. It tangled around her, and she flailed to get free. Her body bashed up against the barred gate. The impact knocked the wind from her.

Happy still had his hand out, but he moved forwards now cautiously, like a tribesman attempting to retrieve a snake. "It's okay, Cher. It's okay. Just stay calm, okay? This was never about you. We're going to get out of here now, I promise?"

Despite his current state of vengefulness, she saw in Happy's eyes that he meant her no harm. She believed him, this had never been about her. Her heart was dubstepping, but she took a long breath and attempted to calm herself. She let out the breath and nodded. "Okay, Happy. Please, just get me out of here."

"I will I promise. Just move away from the—"

The back of Cheryl's head struck the bars, ponytail yanked backwards by an unseen hand. She was still dazed when a slender arm wrapped around her throat. "Open this fucking gate, Happy, or I'll crush her windpipe."

Happy's expression changed from desperation to anger. "Leo, you let her go or I'll take you apart limb by limb."

"Come out here and try, old man."

Cheryl gagged. Her head suddenly felt too small, like her blood was going to burst out of her temples. She wanted to cry out for help, but her throat was closed shut.

"Let her go, Leo. This doesn't involve her."

Leo gave a low, mean chuckle. "Oh, it does now. I might deserve to die, but Cher-bear is innocent. Just like sexy, little Polly was. Oh, Happy, your niece was the best piece of ass I ever had. So tight."

Happy roared and approached the bars. "I'll kill you. I'm

going to tear out your eyes and feed them to you, you sadistic little worm!"

Leo squeezed harder, and Cheryl's arms and legs flapped uncontrollably. "Don't do anything silly, Hap. I say she has less than a minute, but if I keep squeezing, she could—" He made a popping sound "—go anytime. Do you know how much pressure is too much? Let's see."

Cheryl squirmed as the pressure on her throat increased. Along with the pressure was agony, a sharp jolt stabbing her in the centre of her throat. Her head continued shrinking, and she became sure it was going to explode.

Happy put his hands up and nodded profusely. "Okay, Leo. Please, just let her go."

"Unlock the gate."

"Okay, I'm unlocking the gate."

Leo didn't release Cheryl — he was too smart for that — but he did slacken his hold on her slightly. Even that much was a blessed relief. She managed to take half a breath.

Happy reached for the gate and fiddled with the mechanism. It *clicked*.

Cheryl fell forwards, forced by the bars shoving at her back as the gate swung open. Leo rushed inside and threw himself at Happy. He started beating on the older man, but Happy fought back, drumming his fists against Leo's back.

Cheryl could do nothing. Her legs folded beneath her and she sucked at the air, trying to fill her barren lungs. Even though the pressure on her neck had removed itself, she still thought she might die. Her temples pounded like firing cannons.

Leo upended Happy by grabbing his thighs and spilling him onto his back. From on top, he rained down blows. "You stupid fuck," he yelled. "You think you can screw with me? You sad, stupid fuck."

"I'll kill you," said Happy groggily. He was still fighting

back, but most of his energy was being expended on dodging blows. Cheryl had to help him. Leo was too strong, too much younger.

She got onto her hands and knees, wobbling at first, but then managing to steady herself. It was only her will to live that kept her body from giving up. The only thing in the room besides Leo and Happy was the sand. It was everywhere. Instinctively she grabbed at it, feeling safer with her hands full.

Happy's arms dropped to his side, and Leo beat at his unconscious face with both hands. It wouldn't be long before he turned his focus back on her. She had to act fast.

"Hey, little boy!" she yelled.

Leo glanced back over his shoulder. His bloodstained, scowling face was demonic, and it almost caused Cheryl to turn and flee. Instead, she tossed two handfuls of sand right into his face.

Leo howled.

***

Leo clawed at his eyes and wailed. He fell away from Happy and staggered to his feet. The loss of sight had sent him into a panic, and Cheryl knew this was her chance.

But her chance to do what?

Happy was barely conscious, his face a bloody mess. The only real weapon in the tunnel was buried in Monty's skull. She could punch and kick at Leo, but eventually he would shrug off her attacks and grab hold of her again.

Nothing had changed. She was still trapped with no way out.

No, there is *a way out.*

Happy had told her there was an escape hatch in the ceiling. Could she reach it in time? Could she climb out before Leo recovered and came after her?

"You slag. I'm going to make you regret you were ever born." Despite his rage, Leo could only swipe at her blindly. Cheryl dodged out of his range and dared to glance upwards at the open hatch above the chair she had watched Happy die in. Nothing was visible except a crawlspace.

Leo lost his footing in the sand and crashed against one of the perspex walls. He yelped in pain, then released a litany of curses. If he managed to get his hands on her she was done for. He'd tear her apart with his bare hands.

She got moving, climbing up on the chair and stretching for the hatch. It was low enough to reach, but she still had to pull herself up, which would be easier if she stood on the chair's backrest. Even without being a nervous wreck, it was hard to balance, so she almost fell as she attempted it. Somehow she managed it though. The hatch was now at the height of her armpits, low enough to climb into, but just as she began to feel like she might escape, Leo got the sand out of his eyes and grabbed her. He yanked her ankle and she fell hard, fell awkwardly. Her chin struck the back of the chair and her ankle twisted in the uneven sand. The world filled with agony and she went sprawling onto her front, mouth full of blood as she bit through her cheek. She groaned.

Leo was on her immediately. Seeing her ankle was injured, he stamped down and made it hurt even worse. Spikes of hot agony shot up her leg. She screamed.

Leo laughed.

She clutched at more sand, but this time when she threw it Leo turned his head. In response, he kicked her in the head but not hard enough to knock her out — he was a cat batting around a mouse.

"Please don't do this, Leo. Happy is the one who did all this. I-I—"

"Shouldn't be down here, I know. Blah blah blah. Life isn't fair, sweetheart. As much as we think we're gods, we're still just animals. The strong abuse the weak. The confident take from the meek. The lions eat the deer. Sometimes people just die without reason."

Cheryl moaned. "I don't know whether you're deluded or insane. You think you're so powerful? Ha! You have a mid-level office job and no girlfriend. Maybe you believe your own bullshit, Leo, but I see through it. You're just another loser."

Leo roared, and perhaps he did have a lion inside him, but Cheryl couldn't help but see a weasel. Being murdered by a sexual predator was her worst nightmare, and she hated him with every fibre of her being. She also hated herself for letting it happen.

Before he could hurt her again, Cheryl leapt up and scrambled through the open cell door. She hurtled into the centre of the tunnel but almost collapsed as her twisted ankle buckled in protest. Her body felt empty, buzzing with electricity. She managed to shove the pain aside, but it didn't fix her ankle. She wouldn't be able to get away.

Leo tackled her outside the cell that contained the supplies but didn't manage to get a solid hold on her. He snatched at her denim jacket, but she straightened out her arms and let it slide off her. She kept on running, limping. The end of the tunnel loomed ahead. There was nowhere to go. The TVR marked the end of her escape with its sleek headlights like sad eyes. Before she reached the car though, something else caught her attention. A word flashed in her mind. PULL.

She grabbed the lever Monty had first used to light up the tunnel. She sank them into darkness, buying herself some time. It was only a temporary solution but every second was a win.

The TVR's headlights remained on, and they lit up the

tunnel in a pair of disorientating, crisscrossing cones. Cheryl stumbled and struck her hip against the bonnet. Biting down on the pain, she felt her away around the vehicle until she found the handle to the driver's side door.

"You think you can hide from me in the dark?" Leo shouted after her. His silhouette grew in the headlights like a monster from her nightmares. "This only makes it more fun."

Wanting as many barriers between her and Leo as possible, Cheryl yanked open the TVR's door and leapt inside. She slammed it shut and searched desperately for a locking switch. As she frantically pawed at the dashboard controls, her elbow knocked a stalk to the left of the steering wheel. The tunnel flooded with light. Leo yelled and shielded his face with an arm. She had knocked on the high beams. Leo groped blindly, unable to see a thing in the blinding light.

Again, all she had done was buy herself time, but maybe this time she had bought enough.

I have to get back to that hatch.

She opened the car door again and made a bolt for it while Leo was dazed. She skirted around the edge of the headlights and tried to avoid Leo spotting her shifting shadow. It worked, and he completely missed her. In fact, he swore and cursed at her as if she were still inside the car.

Her ankle buckled with every step, the injury growing worse, but she kept on running, would have kept on running on a bloody stump if she had too. She was getting out of there. No way was she going to be a victim of a sadist like Leo. No way was she going to end up like Polly.

She limped back inside the sandy cell just as the lights in the tunnel came back on with a loud *clunk*. Happy was conscious, up on his knees and clutching his head. When he saw her, he immediately lit up. "Cheryl, you're alive!"

Seeing the kindly old man shattered her resolve. All of her defiance and anger fell away and she was once again desperate to be saved. "Help me get out of here, Happy. Help me!"

"Yes, of course." He pointed up at the ceiling hatch. "Come on, climb into the hatch. There should be a ladder you can pull down. Get out of here, Cheryl."

A ladder? Yes, please let there be a ladder.

Happy helped her climb back up onto the chair, and this time she was able to reach inside the hatch and grab hold of something. Whatever it was, it came away easily when she pulled it. A folding ladder slid out of the hatch.

"That's it," said Happy. "Quickly, get up it."

Cheryl dropped the ladder down towards Happy who anchored it in the sand as deeply as he could. It wobbled slightly as Cheryl placed a foot on it, but it was solid enough. She began to hyperventilate, excited by the prospect of freedom.

Leo shouted from out in the tunnel. He had clearly found her missing and was now stalking her. "You think you can run from me bitch?"

Cheryl yelped and covered her mouth. Happy slapped at her thigh. "Go, get out of here."

"What about you?"

"I'm going to deal with the monster that raped my niece."

Cheryl knew there was no argument to be had just by the look on his face — Happy wasn't about to be persuaded. It was now or never, so she placed both feet on the ladder and began to ascend.

Leo rushed into the cell. "Got you, you bitch."

Happy turned to meet him. "Your days of hurting young girls are over."

"You're a dead man." Leo smashed his fist into Happy's face and sent him onto his back. Then he booted the man in the side of his head. Again and again and again. Cheryl didn't know how much trauma the human skull could absorb, but she knew that even if Happy was alive he wasn't getting up to save her.

Leo stopped his vicious assault on Happy and glared up at Cheryl. She had only taken the first two rungs, but she realised now she needed to take more. And quickly.

Leo snatched at her ankle, but this time she was too fast. She scuttled up the ladder and pulled herself up into the crawl space. The mechanism used to release the sand hung above her head, and she struck her temple against its edge. The side of her face grew wet, but she did not care. She shook the pain away and started crawling for her life.

The ladder below rattled as Leo climbed it. He was giving chase. "I'm going to do things to you, Cher, you wouldn't have thought possible. Things you won't even be able to forget when you're dead."

"You're finished, Leo. The truth is out. Everyone will know what a sad little loser you are. You can't get a girl so you have to force yourself on one. The world is going to laugh at you."

Leo roared again, spitting and cursing until his voice cracked. "I'm going to kill you!"

Cheryl had the advantage in the crawl space, she was smaller and had more room to manoeuvre. Her desperate panic also helped propel her along. Ahead of her, the crawl space opened up, and a shaft of light spilled in from somewhere. It was like a beacon of hope. She shuffled herself along, twisted ankle getting stiffer and stiffer as it swelled. It was slowing her down.

"I'm gonna get you, slag. I'm finally going to get you to myself. I told you how this night would end. I told you all along."

Cheryl was too tired to reply to his taunts anymore, so she focused on that shaft of light and kept on moving. Once she reached the light, she discovered another ladder. This one was bolted firmly in place and stretched ten feet upwards through a shaft of wood and soil. At the top she could see the night sky, starlit and clear. Beautiful.

Groaning with pain and exhaustion, she grabbed the first rung and pulled herself forwards. Her face was dripping wet, and she had to wipe herself with a hand. Her fingers came back bloody. Her head was sliced open, but right now it didn't matter. She was alive and had to stay that way.

She took the second rung and began dragging her body upwards and out of the crawl space. Then she was standing again, stepping onto the first rung and climbing.

Leo lunged out of the shadowy crawlspace and into the shaft of light. He grabbed Cheryl's shoe, making her scream. She shook her leg, kicking wildly, then gasped with relief as her trainer slipped off. If she'd been wearing anything tighter he would've had her.

Leo was still confined in the crawlspace, yet to pull himself clear, so Cheryl started up the ladder as fast as she could. It was a massive height to climb when exhausted and wounded, and her swollen ankle had become a lifeless, dead weight hanging off her leg. Yet, she made progress rung by rung.

"You're mine," said Leo, starting up the ladder below her. "All that's waiting for you up there is an empty field. And you only have one leg to run on."

His mocking laughter echoed up the shaft beneath her.

Cheryl started sobbing because she realised he was right. She had a head start, sure, but once she made it out onto open ground he would catch her in seconds. Getting out of this hole didn't mean she was free. There was still nowhere to run. No safety within sight.

Yet all she could do was keep going.

Mum, I'm so sorry. I'm so sorry for abandoning you. For leaving you alone.

Cheryl neared the top of the tunnel, and even though it didn't offer her safety, it filled her heart with hope at the thought of being outside again. At least she wouldn't die buried beneath the ground.

"Just give up," said Leo. "It'll be so much more enjoyable if you open up and accept what's coming to you."

Cheryl grabbed at the next rung, almost at the top. Then she slipped. The blood on her hands dripped and made the metal slick. If she hadn't managed to steady herself just in time, she would have dropped right back down the shaft. A fall high enough to knock the wind out of her and leave her at Leo's mercy.

Due to the slip, Leo was now one rung closer. She still had a head start, for he was battered and bruised as well, but she had to keep moving. Using all of her remaining strength, she propelled herself upwards, praying she did not slip again. One more slip and she was done for.

Leo kept shouting and threatening, but she ignored him. Thoughts of her dad spurred her onward, reminding her that not all men were like Leo, and that her mother needed her to get safely back home.

And I need you too, mum.

She made it to the top, shuddering as the freezing night air slapped her. It was a glorious feeling, like an injection of life. She was back out in the world.

But Leo was right behind her.

If only he would slip and break his back, she thought, wishing that some act of God would save her. But God was a man who had made beasts like Leo. A woman had no choice but to help herself in this cruel world.

The thought struck Cheryl like a bolt of lightning, and she wondered for a moment if God had put it there. Maybe it was the throbbing in her thigh — an ache where the Vaseline tin had pressed against her muscle in the crawl space, or maybe it was the slickness of the blood on her hands.

Cheryl yanked the Vaseline from her pocket and pulled off the lid. She felt stupid, even childish, but this plan was the only one she had. She leaned down inside the shaft, digging her toes into the mud to anchor herself, and got to work. She smothered the top three rungs in the lubricant and a thick helping of her own blood. The slickness of the steel in her hands was satisfying, and her hope began to grow anew.

I'm not going to die out here in the middle of nowhere, you piece of shit.

Cheryl stared down into the dark shaft. Waiting.

Where are you?

Where are you, you son-of-a-bitch?

Leo leapt out of the shadows like a shark escaping the water. He grabbed hold of her wrist, and the sheer weight of him dragged her along the grass on her tummy. She tried to steady herself with her other hand but, ironically, she couldn't get a grip on the slippery rungs. The only thing that kept her from falling headfirst into the shaft was her toes. They had dug a furrow in dirt and anchored her a mere second before gravity had claimed her.

But Leo was still pulling at her arm. He twisted at her wrist, yanking himself upwards so that his face was right next to hers. He snarled at her, hot spittle spattering her cheeks. "I'm gonna shove my cock so far down your throat, you'll have no choice but to swallow."

Cheryl surprised herself by snarling back. "Sorry, loser, I don't swallow. I spit!" She hacked up a mouthful of snot and spat it right into Leo's face. It hit him in the eye and startled him, causing him to instinctively let go of her wrist and try to clear his vision. As he did so, he lost his balance. Letting out a stream of profanity, he reached out to steady himself on a rung. His hand slipped on Vaseline and blood.

The sudden shock caused one of his feet to slip off the rung, and all of a sudden he was swinging by one hand and one foot.

"You bitch! What until I get up there. I'm going to—"

Cheryl rotated onto her butt so that her feet were dangling at the edge of the shaft. She took aim at his burnt hand gripping the rung, the one she had helped patch up earlier. "Shut the fuck up, Leo."

She booted his injured hand with both of her heels. The blow launched Leo backwards and he hit the opposite wall of the shaft. Then he fell.

Cheryl heard the painful crunch ten-feet below and smiled. She leaned forwards, staring into the shaft. The moon glowed just enough to present her the dim, grey image of Leo clutching a badly wounded ankle. Unlike her injury however, this one was no mere sprain. His foot dangled limply from his shin like it wasn't even attached. "Ah, shit, my ankle. It hurts."

"Don't worry," she said. "I'm sure the police will get you some medical attention, asshole."

"I'll kill you. I'm gonna fuck you."

"No thanks. I don't fuck losers."

"You slag."

Cheryl slumped backwards on the cool, caressing grass and closed her eyes. *Yeah*, she thought. *I'm the slag from your nightmares.*

And it's time to wake up. It's over.

But it wasn't. Not yet.

A man approached.

Cheryl sensed the presence behind her, heard the footsteps on the icy grass. She tried to get up, to make a run for it, but she was beat. No more. Whatever horror awaited her, she just wanted it to be over. The best she could do was roll onto her side to see who was there.

She wished she'd kept her eyes closed.

The man without eyes stood in the field, and somehow, despite being blind, he looked down at her. "Are you okay, miss?"

"Never been better. If you're going to kill me, can you please make it quick?"

The strange man muttered something over his shoulder and someone else appeared. It shocked Cheryl enough that she managed to sit up. This second man also possessed no eyes, and was dressed in a white cloak matching that of the other man. The newcomer handed Cheryl a flask of water, which she drank from greedily. Then he stepped away, leaving the original stranger to deal with her.

Gasping from having gulped so much, Cheryl looked up at the grotesque man and asked, "W-Who are you?"

With a slight grin, the man lifted his arms to either side of him and a dozen figures shifted in the darkness. All of them had no eyes. "We are Justice, and tonight it has been served."

"I..." She wondered how many times she had said this particular line today, but she wanted very much to reiterate it once more. "I'm not meant to be here."

"Indeed, you are not." The eyeless stranger offered her a hand, and she surprised herself by taking it. His palm was warm, and it made her suddenly realise how freezing it was out there in the night. As if having read her mind, another stranger appeared and wrapped her in a blanket.

"You're not going to hurt me?" she asked.

"Do you deserve to be hurt, miss?"

"I... I don't think so."

"Then we shall assume you do not."

Cheryl looked back at the hole in the ground. She could hear Leo still swearing down in the shaft. He didn't know there were other people here — and probably still hoped to rape and murder her.

"He shall be dealt with shortly," said the man with no eyes, somehow seeing where she was looking. "We should move away."

He started walking, white cloak flowing behind him, so she stumbled after him. Her ankle felt like it was made out of wood. "What are you going to do with me? I witnessed everything."

"What do you propose we do with you?"

"Um, let me go?"

"Then we shall let you go."

Cheryl studied the man's face, then decided it was impossible to read someone without any eyes. "What's to stop me telling people about everything I saw tonight?"

"Nothing. You may tell. You will not be believed."

"Why not?"

"Because there will be no evidence of this night. People will think you insane."

"Um, there's a giant torture chamber under the ground. That's enough evidence as far as I'm concerned."

The eyeless man stopped, and she suddenly cursed herself for irritating him. Why was she so intent on arguing with a disfigured man who had just killed six of her co-workers? Was she crazy? Despite her fears, the man didn't strike her or attempt to kill her. Instead, he pointed. "Losing Happy was a great failure on our part, as was your arrival, yet all must be put right. You may wish to look away for this part."

Cheryl frowned, and it wasn't until she felt the ground vibrate that she looked back towards the hole. What looked like a petrol tanker began backing up towards the shaft, and she watched in horror as a team assembled and opened up a valve at the vehicle's rear. Petrol cascaded into the hole, causing Leo to shout and curse even louder from below. At first he sounded startled and confused, but then he panicked. "Please, Cher! Don't do this. Don't burn me."

Cheryl gasped. "He thinks I'm the one doing this. He thinks I'm going to burn him alive."

The man with no eyes smiled. "An ironic twist, don't you agree."

"You can't do this! You don't have the right."

"Justice needs no right. And it is done."

One of the other eyeless men threw a lit match into the hatch and hurried away as an inferno took ahold beneath the ground. Leo's screams hurtled towards the stars, making Cheryl weep, not for the victim, but that such an amount of pain could exist in the universe. His howls went on for several minutes.

More vehicles started to arrive. Cheryl recognised a digger, and what looked like a cement mixer. There was also a small crane.

"The containers shall be dug up and removed," said the man with no eyes. "Then the hole shall be filled. It may look suspicious, but that is all it will be. No one in authority will make a fuss, they never do."

Cheryl shook her head, trying to understand. Then she did. "You have people working for you in the police. The government?"

"Justice rules all. You shall remain in our care until the site is made good. Then you may return home, unmolested."

"Unharmed? Ha! I'm going to need therapy for the rest of my life. Not to mention the company I work for has just been murdered."

The eyeless man shook his head like her dad had used to whenever he thought she was being cheeky. "You shall be made whole. Three years of whatever salary you are on, up front."

Cheryl balked, doing rough numbers in her head. "Wow that's, um, not nothing."

"And yet it is." The eyeless man turned to face her fully now, and he sighed, as if fed up with the very entirety of the world. "Use the money wisely, miss. Live a good life, one for yourself and for others. Fail to do so and we could meet again."

"I promise. Only the straight and narrow for me. I mean, I wouldn't do something as horrible as trapping people in a hole and killing them."

"A debt was paid tonight. Judgement was passed. You may keep yours. Go with my colleagues and attempt to remain quiet." The eyeless man walked away, replaced by another almost identical. Within a few seconds, it was impossible to tell who she had been talking to. They all looked the same. Several dozen eyeless men now milled about the field in their white cloaks, busily taking care of the situation. The one nearest to her ushered her away, leading her to safety. Safety in a world where Justice was an army of eyeless men dispensing justice to the unrighteous via deadly games.

This was not the weekend she'd expected.

NOON

Cheryl took the Prosecco from the fridge and placed it down on the kitchen table. Her mother looked at her in confusion. "It's a little early, love."

"Not today it's not. We're celebrating."

"We are?"

"Yep. It's a Friday afternoon, and you and me are going to spend the day getting blotto and watching *Grey's Anatomy.*"

Her mother shifted uncomfortably. This was something Cheryl's father would never have approved of. "Oh, Cheryl, I don't think—"

"Mum, stop worrying, okay? Dad is gone. I miss him as much as you do, but he's gone. It's okay for us to be happy without him, and it's okay for us to do things that we want to do, even if it's not something he would have enjoyed when he was alive. If you want to go on a year long cruise and sleep with a Greek waiter, then do it, mum. Dad's gone, but we're still here. I'm still here, and I want to see you happy. I want us both to enjoy being alive. Because that's what dad would really have wanted for us."

Tears formed in her mother's eyes, and Cheryl hoped it

was because her words were hitting home. No more being afraid of living. Life was too short. Her nightmare underground had shown her that.

The strange army of eyeless men had held her captive for another five hours after her ordeal in the tunnel, releasing her shortly before the sun had begun to rise along the edges of the field. They handed her back her phone and wallet, then disappeared in a fleet of black vans. For a while, she had just stood there alone, waiting for the sun to rise fully. Once daylight arrived, she felt safe enough to move, and she limped back to the hay barns. All three cars had been removed, John's Bentley, Monty's Range Rover, and Leo's Mazda. There was no evidence anyone had ever been there at all.

She then hobbled along for another two hours until she found a small village. There, she entered a tiny newsagent and asked the assistant for the number of a taxi. It was an expensive ride that she was forced to pay for upfront. Muddy, bloodstained, and limping, she wasn't someone the taxi driver was willing to drive an hour out of town for on trust. She was happy to pay up front, so long as he didn't ask questions. The entire journey took place in silence.

When Cheryl had arrived home — something she had feared would never happen — her mother was busy in the kitchen, which meant she had a chance to run up the stairs and get changed quickly. Her mother had been concerned to hear her upstairs, but Cheryl's 'happy' act had been enough to dispel her fears. She'd simply been dying for the toilet, she had explained, and needed to dash upstairs so as not to make a smell. Her mother had clucked her tongue and said, "I told you not to eat the food."

Nobody opened up the Alscon offices on Monday morning. Or Tuesday. Or for the rest of the week. Eventually the police were informed that something was amiss and they came to ask their questions. Cheryl couldn't believe how few they had. *Have you seen John Alscon recently? When? Did he seem strange? Guilty or suicidal?* The questions were all leading, and Cheryl knew enough to play along and answer in the way the investigators wanted. They were wrapping things up with as little fuss as possible.

A few days later, the evidence of Polly's death came out. Audio snippets, DNA, and secret camera footage painted a picture of Happy, aggrieved uncle exposing a conspiracy of rape and murder. Leo, John, Monty, and Alfie had raped and murdered Polly while Maggie watched. Knowing they were heading for prison, they had cleared Alscon's accounts and gone into hiding. It was suspected that they had dealt with Happy too in an attempt to silence him — his body had been found beaten to a pulp in John's office. The newspapers referred to them all as the *The Tile Gang*. Not particularly inspired, but that was a good thing because the entire ghoulish incident was forgotten within a month. The only person Cheryl felt bad for was Monty. He had been painted as a rapist and murderer, when in actual fact he was only a thief. It wasn't justice as far as she was concerned.

Her bank account had swelled with mystery funds that she chose not to question. It was almost enough to buy a flat, or even get a low mortgage on a house. A nest egg that she couldn't help but keep staring at on her banking app. Each time she logged in she expected it to be gone.

"I've been accepted back at university," she told her mother now as she began uncorking the Prosecco. "They're going to let me continue from where I left off. I could have my degree within two years. Isn't that great?"

Her mother's face fell. "What about work? How will you pay your bills?"

"Don't worry, mum. We all got redundancy money after Alscon was sold off. I'm good for a while. I'll get a part time job to tide me over."

Her mother stared down at the table, clasping her hands together. "I suppose that means you'll move into halls again. When do you leave?"

"I'm not leaving, mum. I'll get myself a cheap car and I'll travel to uni. You don't have to worry about me leaving yet, okay, but you do need to get back on your feet because I won't be here forever. One of these days, I'd like to meet someone." She smiled. "To have what you and dad had."

Her mother's face was a mixture of emotions, but she reached forward and took Cheryl's hands. "I hope you have all that and more, sweetheart. I'm sorry these last couple of years have been so hard on you, but I'm proud of the woman you've become. I suppose I need to find out what kind of woman, I am now that your dad's gone. I've been too afraid to find out."

"You're my mum, and I love you." She leant forward and wiped a tear from her mother's cheek. "Come on, let's go put our pyjamas back on like we used to when I was a kid. We can start life again on Monday."

"You don't want to spend the entire weekend with your silly old, mum."

Cheryl popped the cork. "I do, mum. In fact, I couldn't think of anything better. Meet you in the living room in five?"

Her mother smiled and got up. "I'll get some nibbles."

"Deal."

Cheryl headed up to her bedroom to get changed. She couldn't believe she ever hated being stuck at home during the weekends. Excitement was overrated.

Her pyjamas were laid out on her bed, which was strange because she remembered dumping them in a pile on the floor. It didn't worry her too much because her short term memory had been all over the place recently. Just one of many symptoms of her trauma. She hadn't been kidding about needing therapy, and every night she awoke from strange and disturbing dreams. People had died right in front of her, and she wasn't going to wipe that from her mind any time soon.

She started kicking off her jeans, ready to get back into something more comfortable. She reached out for her pyjamas but then froze. Nestled underneath her top was a sheet of paper. This time she was sure she had not placed it there. Somebody else had. Somebody had been inside her room.

She picked up the piece of paper and examined it. It took her a while to figure it out, but it seemed to be a medical report. It had her father's name on it, and when she checked the date, she saw the examination had taken place a few weeks before he had died. It listed several things, but what jumped out at her was the doctor's comments that her father's health was good, and the ratings for blood pressure and cholesterol. Both were fine. Both were healthy.

What did it mean?

Who had put this in her room?

Then she saw it. Written on the back of the photocopy was a message.

JUSTICE DEMANDS THE TRUTH.

JUST SAY YES.

Cheryl looked around her room but saw nothing else out of the ordinary. "Yes," she said, and then louder, "Yes!"

A few minutes later she went downstairs to join her mother, and to wait for Justice.

It would arrive soon.

PLEA FROM THE AUTHOR

Hey, Reader. So you got to the end of my book. I hope that means you enjoyed it. Whether or not you did, I would just like to thank you for giving me your valuable time to try and entertain you. I am truly blessed to have such a fulfilling job, but I only have that job because of people like you; people kind enough to give my books a chance and spend their hard-earned money buying them. For that I am eternally grateful.

If you would like to find out more about my other books then please visit my website for full details. You can find it at:

http://www.iainrobwright.com.

Also feel free to contact me on Facebook, Twitter, or email (all details on the website), as I would love to hear from you.

If you enjoyed this book and would like to help, then you could think about leaving a review on Amazon, Goodreads, or anywhere else that readers visit. The most important part of how well a book sells is how many positive reviews it has, so if you leave me one then you are directly helping me to continue on this journey as a fulltime writer. Thanks in advance to anyone who does. It means a lot.

WANT FREE BOOKS?

Don't miss out on your FREE Iain Rob Wright horror starter pack. Five free bestselling horror novels sent straight to your inbox. No strings attached.

For more information just visit this page:
www.iainrobwright.com

Iain has more than a dozen novels available to purchase right now.

- **Animal Kingdom**
- **AZ of Horror**
- **2389**
- **Holes in the Ground** (with J.A.Konrath)
- **Sam**
- **ASBO**
- **The Final Winter**
- **The Housemates**
- **Sea Sick** FREE!
- **Ravage**
- **Savage**
- **The Picture Frame**
- **Wings of Sorrow**
- **The Gates**
- **Legion**
- **Extinction**
- **TAR**
- **House Beneath the Bridge**
- **The Peeling**
- **Blood on the bar**

SARAH STONE THRILLER SERIES

- **Soft Target** FREE!
- **Hot Zone**
- **End Play**

Iain Rob Wright is one of the UK's most successful horror and suspense writers, with novels including the critically acclaimed, THE FINAL WINTER; the disturbing bestseller, ASBO; and the wicked screamfest, THE HOUSEMATES.

His work is currently being adapted for graphic novels, audio books, and foreign audiences. He is an active member of the Horror Writer Association and a massive animal lover.

www.iainrobwright.com
FEAR ON EVERY PAGE

For more information
www.iainrobwright.com
iain.robert.wright@hotmail.co.uk

Made in the
USA
Columbia, SC